Margaret Daley, an award-winning author of ninety books (five million sold worldwide), has been married for over forty years and is a firm believer in romance and love. When she isn't traveling, she's writing love stories, often with a suspense thread, and corralling her three cats, who think they rule her household. To find out more about Margaret, visit her website at margaretdaley.com.

Debby Giusti is an award-winning Christian author who met and married her military husband at Fort Knox, Kentucky. Together they traveled the world, raised three wonderful children and have now settled in Atlanta, Georgia, where Debby spins tales of mystery and suspense that touch the heart and soul. Visit Debby online at debbygiusti.com; blog with her at seekerville.blogspot.com and craftieladiesofromance.blogspot.com; and email her at debby@debbygiusti.com.

CHRISTMAS PERIL

MARGARET DALEY
DEBBY GIUSTI

HARLEQUIN® LOVE INSPIRED® SUSPENSE

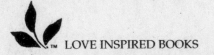

LOVE INSPIRED BOOKS

Recycling programs
for this product may
not exist in your area.

ISBN-13: 978-0-373-78958-0

Christmas Peril

Copyright © 2009 by Harlequin Books S.A.

The publisher acknowledges the copyright holders
of the individual works as follows:

Merry Mayhem
Copyright © 2009 by Margaret Daley

Yule Die
Copyright © 2009 by Deborah W. Giusti

www.Harlequin.com

Printed in U.S.A.

CONTENTS

MERRY MAYHEM   9
Margaret Daley

YULE DIE   167
Debby Giusti

MERRY MAYHEM

Margaret Daley

To Aubrey with all my love

Trust in the Lord with all thine heart; and lean not unto thine own understanding. In all thy ways acknowledge Him, and He shall direct thy paths.
—Proverbs 3:5-6

Chapter One

Annie Coleman almost dropped the phone at her ex-boyfriend's words, but she couldn't. She had to keep it together for her daughter. Jayden played nearby, oblivious to the sheer terror Annie was feeling at hearing Bryan's gasping warning. "Run. Disappear... Don't trust anyone, especially the police."

A scuffling noise on the other end of the phone sent her heartbeat slamming against her chest. What was going on? A swishing sound filled her ears, followed by something like a fist hitting flesh and a groan that iced her blood.

"Thought you could get away," a gruff voice said between punches. "You haven't finished telling me what I need to know."

Annie panicked. What was going on? What

was happening to Bryan on the other end? Confusion gripped her in a choke hold, her chest tightening with each inhalation.

"I don't want—" Bryan's rattling gasp punctuated the brief silence "—any money. Just let me go. I'll—" a smack interrupted his words "—forget…everything."

"I'm not worried about you telling a soul." The menace in the assailant's tone underscored his deadly intent. "Now all I need is where you hid it exactly. If you tell me now, it will be a lot less painful."

"I can't—" Agony laced each word.

"What's that? A phone?"

The sounds of a struggle then a gunshot blasted her eardrum. Curses roared through the connection.

Fear paralyzed Annie in the middle of her kitchen. *Was Bryan shot? Dead?* she screamed silently, clutching the receiver until her fingers locked into place.

"Who's this? Annie? Who are you?"

The assailant's voice so clear on the phone panicked her. She slammed it down onto its cradle as though that action could sever the memories from her mind. But nothing would. Had she just heard her daughter's father being killed? What information did Bryan have?

How did that man know her name? Question after question bombarded her from all sides, but inertia held her still.

The ringing of the phone jarred her out of a trance. She zoomed in on the lighted panel on the receiver and noted the call was from Bryan's cell. The assailant now had her home telephone number! He could discover where she lived. He knew what she'd heard.

The last time she'd talked with Bryan early this morning, he was finally paying his father a visit for the first time. What could have gone wrong with that? Why was he warning her? What was Bryan sorry about? What did he do? Why shouldn't she trust the police? The questions started all over again, slamming one after another into her thoughts.

"Mommy, what's wrong?"

Looking up at Jayden, Annie schooled her features into what she hoped was a calm expression while her stomach reeled. "You know I've been thinking, honey? We need to take a vacation. We've been working so hard this year. It's time for us to have…an adventure." Her daughter was all into having adventures, since her favorite book series was *The Brandon Twins' Escapades*.

"Where?" Jayden came to her and threw her arms around Annie.

She wished she could stay forever holding her child, pretending she hadn't heard what she had. But she couldn't.

Annie hugged her daughter to her, then leaned back. "That's a surprise—a Christmas surprise." Because she wasn't sure herself, but she couldn't get Jayden's father's words out of her mind. *Run. Disappear. Don't trust anyone, especially the police.* Nor would she forget the gunfire that followed.

Grief and fear swamped her. Although she and Bryan had never married and were only friends for Jayden's sake, he'd tried to do right by his daughter in his own way. Had that led to him doing something foolish? Deadly?

"When are we going?" Jayden stepped back from Annie.

"Right now is as good a time as any. It's Saturday. I'll get some money and then we'll hit the road."

Jayden whirled from her and started across the kitchen. "Wait till Mandy hears I'm going on an adventure."

"We don't have time for you to call Mandy." They might not have much time for anything. She didn't even know where Bryan had been calling her from. "I'll get our suitcases. Let's see how fast we can pack. Take only your favorite things." Although she tried to make it sound like a game, her voice quavered, and Annie curled her trembling hands until her fingernails dug into her palms.

At the door her daughter paused, cocking her head. "When will we be coming back?"

Not until I figure out what's going on. I can't take the risk that Bryan has gotten caught up in some scheme and somehow involved us. He'd done some foolish, impulsive things in the past. "I'm not sure. But we'll probably be gone for a few weeks." She hoped only that long.

Jayden whirled around. "Then I'll need my new doll and my treasure chest."

The memory of when Bryan had given his daughter an antique porcelain doll for her birthday last month jolted Annie as though she'd stuck her finger into a socket. He'd even given them his mother's family's Bible, a surprise, since he wasn't a Christian, but he'd wanted his daughter to have it when she got older. Would Jayden ever see her father again?

Annie passed the sign for Christmas, Oklahoma. After two days on the road, driving long hours and crashing at night, she needed a place to stay for a while to figure out what was going on. She didn't even know if Bryan was dead or alive or where he'd been when he'd called her.

"I'm tired, Mommy."

"We're almost there."

She prayed that her mother's cousin, one she hadn't seen in fifteen years, still lived in Christmas. After racking her brain, she'd finally come up with Sara McLain's place as a possible refuge until she did some investigating and came up with a plan. Fond memories of a holiday season spent in a town called Christmas kept creeping into her thoughts as she drove toward Oklahoma.

In the motel rooms along the way, she'd spent each night after Jayden had gone to sleep reading Bryan's mother's family Bible, looking for guidance on what to do. But the Lord hadn't answered her prayers in years. So why had she thought He would now?

On the outskirts of Christmas, Annie stopped at Speedy Mart to get some gas and directions to her cousin's house. As she filled her tank, Jayden danced around, happy to be out of the car.

"Honey, stay right next to me." Annie envisioned the unknown assailant on the other end of the phone call suddenly appearing and grabbing her and her daughter. Would she ever feel safe again?

She searched her surroundings, looking for anyone who appeared suspicious. A car pulled in behind her, and a man got out to get gas. Didn't she see that Chevy behind her on Interstate 40 back a hundred miles? Not sure, she massaged her temples, trying to rid herself of the constant fear that had engrained itself in her.

When she was through filling her tank, she took Jayden's hand and hurried toward the building to pay. A bell rang as she opened the door. She glanced back at the man finishing up putting gas into his car. He caught her gaze, grinned and got back into his Chevy, then pulled out of Speedy Mart. Relief slumped her shoulders. False alarm—she hoped.

At the counter she started to pull out her credit card out of habit, but she stopped herself and instead withdrew some cash from her quickly dwindling savings. She smiled at the older woman who took her money and gave her change.

"You just passing through?"

"No," Annie said, stuffing the dollars into her purse, her gaze slanting toward her daughter, who was holding her porcelain doll and exploring the candy rack next to the counter. When she fingered one, Annie said, "Jayden, no candy right now."

"But I'm hungry."

"We'll get something in a little bit."

"Here visiting?" the attendant asked and slid her cash drawer closed.

"Yes." Behind Annie the bell over the door jingled, and she automatically turned to see who was entering. For the past two days she'd been constantly looking over her shoulder and checking out all the cars behind her on the highway. She'd never been paranoid before, but fear was taking over her life.

A tall man in a navy-blue police uniform came into the store and grinned at the woman behind the counter. Annie breathed a sigh. Then she remembered Bryan's warning, and tension whipped through her.

The police officer's gaze swept the store as though checking to make sure everything was all right before settling first on Jayden then Annie. The sharp, assessing look moved down her length before coming back to her face. A smile crinkled the corners of his cobalt-blue eyes and lit their depths with a glitter. He nodded a greeting toward her.

Uncomfortable with his scrutiny, Annie

turned her attention back to the cashier. "I need directions to Sara McLain's house on Bethlehem Street. Do you know her?" She was over a thousand miles from Crystal Creek. This man had nothing to do with what had happened in Florida.

The older woman glanced behind Annie.

"Maybe I can help you." The police officer stepped up to the counter a few feet from Annie. "Sara's a neighbor of mine."

"Oh, good, you know where she lives. My name is Annie Madison." Which was true but Madison was her middle name. She'd decided the first night on the road that was the name she would go by as a precaution in case anyone was looking for Annie Coleman.

"I'm Caleb Jackson, the police chief of Christmas." He offered his hand.

She fit hers in his and shook it. "Nice to meet you. Can you give me directions to Sara's?" Annie snagged her daughter before she wandered toward another rack with chips. "I'm her cousin."

"Cousin?" Skepticism sounded in his voice. "She's always talking about her family. I don't remember her mentioning you."

"It's been a while since I've seen her." She hated explaining herself to a stranger, but she didn't need the police chief becoming suspicious.

A grin eased the wariness from his expression. "Sara will be thrilled. She was just talking about how none of her nieces or nephews could come for Christmas. Have you ever been here?"

"Yes, the last time was when I was ten during the holidays, but I don't remember much about the town, except all the lights downtown and the huge Christmas tree in the park." She glanced out the large picture window, a blanket of clouds darkening the late afternoon. "I need to talk with Sara this evening and then find a place to stay. My daughter is tired and hungry." She hoped Sara would let her stay with her, but she hadn't seen her in years and she might not open her home to her. If that were the case, she didn't know what she would do. Her money was limited. Fear, always present since she'd last heard from Bryan, wormed its way deeper into her mind.

"Sara fell a few weeks ago. She could use some help around the house, but she hates asking anyone to. Maybe you are an answer to a prayer. I'll show you where she lives. You can follow me." He turned to the lady behind the counter. "I just need a cup of your coffee, Marge."

"Already have it for you." The woman took the dollar the police chief set on the counter.

"Ready, Mrs. Madison?" He snatched up the cup.

"It's Ms. Madison. I'm not married."

She'd never been married. Although Bryan and she had discussed marriage when she discovered she was pregnant in college, she'd decided against it when he was arrested for driving under the influence. Too many red flags kept popping up in their relationship. When she'd met him as a freshman, he was an upperclassman with arresting blue eyes and an easy smile. He'd whisked her off her feet, and she'd given herself to him. She deeply regretted her choice back then, but one good thing had come from it: Jayden.

Taking her daughter's hand, she started for the door. "I appreciate you showing me where Sara lives. I probably could have wandered around until I stumbled onto Bethlehem. I remember what a big deal the holidays are here in Christmas."

"Yeah, the town grows at this time of year. We get people from all over Oklahoma and the surrounding states visiting during the season. We go all out."

"The thing I mainly recall is the festival of lights," Annie said as she helped Jayden into the back and slipped behind the steering wheel of her ten-year-old Ford Mustang.

"We added fireworks about twelve years ago." He shut her door and strode toward his police cruiser.

As she followed Caleb Jackson through the town, holiday spirit was evident everywhere she looked. Every street's name had a Christmas theme: Noel Avenue, Candy Cane Lane, Mistletoe Street, Nativity Road. Usually Christmas had little meaning for her. She only celebrated it for Jayden's sake.

Although Bryan tried to help as much as he could, it had been a struggle supporting her daughter on an office manager's salary. She was thankful when she called her employer, Ron Adams, that he'd been understanding about her suddenly taking some time off. She'd been with him for five years, and this was a slow time of the year for his roofing business. She hoped by the first of the year that she could go back to Crystal Creek and her old life. She wanted to believe that Bryan was all right and there had been no reason for her to flee.

Six blocks off the main street through downtown where one store after another dealing with Christmas edged the thoroughfare on both sides, the police chief turned onto Bethlehem. Large houses—some Victorian, all decorated for Christmas—lined the street.

He stopped in front of one of the Victorian homes, painted a powder-blue, with a black wrought-iron fence along the sidewalk. The lot Sara McLain's place sat on was at least half an acre. In fact, all the houses on the street had sizeable yards. Memories of running and playing on the lawn flashed into her thoughts. She remembered feeling safe here.

Annie stared at the three-story structure with a Christmas tree positioned in the center of a floor-to-ceiling window facing the street. White lights draped the pine with gold bows and white ornaments. "We're here. Remember, your last name is Madison, honey. It's important you don't forget."

"Why, Mommy?"

She didn't want to tell her daughter the reason, but she had to say something or she would continue to ask. "That's our new last name now. We're on an adventure and in disguise."

"Oh, great!" Jayden unsnapped her seat belt and hopped from the car, hugging her doll.

As Annie climbed out, she heard Caleb Jackson introduce himself and ask her daughter, "What's your name?"

Annie stiffened, gripping the door handle.

"Jayden Madison."

Annie expelled a deep breath and rounded the front of her Mustang. She knew he was a police chief, but the words *don't trust anyone, especially the police* had kept her up most of the past two nights, listening to every sound passing her motel room door.

His gaze captured hers. "This is Sara's."

"Yeah, I remember playing here, making—" Annie pointed toward a spot in the front yard "—a snowman right there."

"A snowman. I wanna make one." Jayden looked up at the sky. "When's it gonna snow?"

Caleb chuckled. "In Oklahoma, if you don't like the weather, just stick around a day. It most likely will change. But right now, there isn't any snow forecasted."

Jayden's mouth turned down in a pout. "I was hoping for snow. I've never seen any."

He winked at her little girl. "Maybe while you're visiting, there will be some." When he shifted toward Annie, Caleb gestured down the street. "I don't live far from here. The last house at the end of the block."

"Thanks for showing us where Sara lived."

Taking her daughter's hand, she started to open the gate that led into the front yard, when the police chief reached around her and swung it toward him. His arm brushed up against hers. Jolted by the contact, she stepped back, aware of the man only inches from her. His smile encompassed his whole face and made his eyes gleam.

But she'd learned the hard way to be wary of strangers. Look what happened when she'd given into Bryan and his smooth-talking ways. She would love to trust the police chief with what was going on in her life, but at the moment she didn't even know what that was. In a tight crunch she would appreciate someone like Caleb Jackson watching out for her. She hoped she never had to find out just how good he would be defending someone. The very thought sent a shiver down her.

"Cold?"

She nodded, although her chill had nothing to do with the weather.

"It's getting nippy. So, Jayden, you might get that snow after all. I've learned not to take the forecasters too seriously." He mounted the stairs to the porch that wrapped around one side of the house and pressed the bell. "It'll take Sara a bit to get to the door." He leaned back against the wall, crossing his arms. "What do you think of our little town?"

"I've never seen so many Christmas decorations in one place."

He quirked a grin. "Yeah, it does take some getting used to for newcomers. We go all out for a good three months a year. Personally, I like what Christmas stands for. We could use it year round."

"What? Rampant commercialism?"

He laughed, a warm sound that Annie responded to. "A cynic. Before you pass judgment on the town, you need to experience the holidays here." He straightened as the door opened. "And I wasn't talking about the commercialism of Christmas but the celebration of Christ's birth. It all started something awesome."

All words fled Annie's mind at his answer. She hadn't expected it. But the appearance of her cousin in the entrance gave her a reprieve from making any comment.

A small woman, about five feet, her totally white hair pulled back in a bun, pushed open the screen and smiled at the police chief.

"Goodness, I didn't expect you for another hour, Caleb."

"I'm not here to fix the leak in the sink, but I'll be back later to take care of it. Right now I brought you Annie and Jayden Madison." He gestured to each of them when he said their names.

Sara's gaze took both she and her child in, a puzzled expression on her face.

"I'm your cousin. Alice's daughter." Annie held her breath, hoping Sara remembered.

"Ah, it's been years since I've seen you or your mother. How is Alice?"

"She died seven years ago."

"Oh, I'm sorry to hear that. We lost touch when y'all moved to Miami." Her forehead wrinkled in thought, Sara studied Annie with a sharp alertness in her brown eyes. Then she swept her attention to Annie's daughter. "What an adorable little girl. You and your mother look a lot alike. I think I've got photos from her visit when she was a little girl. If I can find them, I'll show you." She grinned at Jayden and stepped to the side. "Come in. It's getting cold." After Annie and Jayden entered, Sara asked Caleb, "Coming in?"

"No, I have to get back to the station." The

police chief peered at Annie, who stood next to Sara in the entrance. "Nice meeting y'all."

When her cousin closed the door, she faced Annie. "Hon, what brought you to Christmas, Oklahoma?"

Annie's stomach constricted, her grip on her daughter's hand tightening. She didn't know how to answer Sara. The woman's kind eyes made her long to share what happened, but words refused to take hold in Annie's mind. How could she explain anything to Sara when she herself didn't understand? This was her problem, not Sara's. She'd always managed on her own in the past. This would be no different.

Sara waved her hand. "When you're ready, you'll tell me." Then using her cane, she headed toward the room off to the right of the foyer. "Come in, and make yourself at home."

Annie remained rooted to the floor.

Finally Jayden tugged on her hand. "Mommy, okay?"

Annie blinked and glanced down at her daughter—her whole life. Everything she did she did for Jayden. If they were in danger, she had to protect her daughter at all costs. "Yes, I'm fine. Let's go see what Miss Sara has to say."

"We could tell her we're on an adventure."

"Let's keep that a secret between us." Annie placed her forefinger over her lips.

Jayden pulled her down so she could whisper, "This house is *big*."

"Yeah, it is. I bet there are great hiding places in here." She just hoped she never had to use them.

Chapter Two

As Annie checked the meat loaf and placed the vegetable casserole in the oven, the door-bell rang. Jayden was so absorbed in her new coloring book she didn't even notice when Annie hurried from the kitchen.

Earlier she and Sara had talked and the older woman had shown Jayden the photos of Annie as a little girl and then given her one to put in her treasure chest. Annie had volunteered to cook dinner. Although Sara was a relative and had opened her home to her gladly, she wouldn't freeload off her. She was determined to help her cousin as much as possible in exchange for giving her a place where she could decide about her future.

A few seconds later, she swung the door open to the police chief standing on the porch

with a puzzled expression creasing his forehead. His gaze locked on hers.

"Did something happen?" she asked, trying
not to react to the man. But for some reason her
heartbeat accelerated, and it really had nothing to do with the assessing look he sent her.
Although no longer in his uniform, the man
commanded a person's attention even wearing
jeans and an Oklahoma University sweatshirt.

His features smoothed into a grin. "No, just
surprised to find you here."

"You are? You brought me here."

"Yeah, I did," he said in a thoughtful tone.
"Your car isn't out front."

"I parked it around back by the detached
garage." No sense leaving it on the street for
anyone looking for her to find. Little by little
she was trying to learn caution, but she'd never
even watched a crime show on TV or read a
suspense book.

"When I didn't see it, I thought maybe you'd
left."

"Nope. Sara insisted Jayden and I stay with
her through the holidays. Come in." Annie
opened the door wider and stepped to the side.
"Sara's in the living room resting her eyes, she
says, but I think she's really taking a nap."

Caleb entered with his toolbox. "Ah, in her

lounge chair, which she calls her command post." He sniffed the air. "You're cooking dinner?"

"Yes, meat loaf."

"It smells great." He followed Annie to the kitchen. "What are you coloring, Jayden?" Stopping next to the table, he peered over her daughter's shoulder. "You like animals?"

"Yes. We were gonna get a puppy for Christmas. I guess we won't since we're on an adven—" Jayden's gaze flew to Annie, and her daughter snapped her mouth closed.

Caleb glanced from her daughter to Annie. For a few seconds his forehead crinkled as though trying to come up with the right question to ask. Then a smile leaked back into his expression as he turned his attention to Jayden. "I have a dog. Ralph is a mutt and loves children. You'll have to come visit him. He's deaf, which doesn't make him a good watchdog, so I'm glad not much happens around here."

Jayden twisted around in her chair and looked at Annie. "Can I see Ralph? I can finish coloring later."

Annie laughed. "Honey, I think Mr. Jackson means some other day. He's here to fix a leak."

Her daughter's pout descended. "We aren't home now for me to get my puppy."

"We'll get a puppy later." When she knew what was going on and she had a game plan. Tomorrow she needed to go somewhere and use a computer. Maybe if she surfed around, she could discover what had happened to Bryan.

"I'll bring Ralph down tomorrow for you to meet him." Caleb put his toolbox on the floor in front of the sink. "Will I interfere with you cooking dinner?"

"No, I just finished preparing the meal right before you came. Great timing."

"I aim to please. Don't let me stop you from doing whatever you need to do." He knelt on the floor and opened the cabinet door, then reached in.

Annie sat next to Jayden, trying her best to ignore the police chief's presence. Taking up the crayon nearest her, she started to color until her daughter said, "A cat isn't blue."

Annie glanced down at the paper and noticed what she'd done. "Oh, you're right. Sorry, honey."

A commotion behind her drew her attention to Caleb. He took a wrench to the faucet, his movements a study in economical action. Transfixed for a moment, she watched until he peered back at her. One corner of his mouth tilted up, a gleam in his startlingly dark blue eyes. She'd always had a thing for blue eyes. Bryan's had been—were—blue.

Over the years her ex-boyfriend had schemed to get rich, tired of being poor, not supporting his daughter as he wanted. Going to meet his wealthy father had been his latest ploy to get rich quick. His mother's death six weeks ago had affected Bryan. Before she'd passed away from a heart attack, he'd thought his father was dead. Not long afterward, he'd discovered he was very much alive and had lots of money. He'd intended to reintroduce himself and benefit from his father's wealth. He'd never gotten the chance to tell her what had come of that meeting.

"I'm partial to blue," Caleb said with a wink, drawing Annie back to the present.

Heat scored her cheeks, and she quickly returned to the paper between her and Jayden. This time she noticed the crayon she selected, making sure it was an appropriate color.

It was only because she was in unfamiliar surroundings with an unknown future stretching before her and Jayden that her nerves were frazzled. Caleb had nothing to do with the fact that her hand quivered as she grasped the crayon and tried to color within the lines and was not succeeding very well.

"I think that should take care of the leak," Caleb said as he closed the cabinet door under the sink.

Annie knew the exact second he stood behind her and looked over her shoulder. His spicy scent vied with the aromas of the cooking meat loaf and vegetable casserole.

He pointed to the blue kitten left abandoned on the page. "There are some cats with a bluish tint to their fur."

"There are?" Jayden's green eyes widened.

"Yeah, Harriet, the receptionist at the station, owns one."

"Can I see it?"

"I'll say something to Harriet and see what I can come up with—that is, if it's okay with your mother." Caleb moved to sit in the chair next to Annie at the oak table.

"That's fine." Annie slid her gaze away from Caleb's. "So should we finish coloring the kitten blue?"

Her daughter giggled. "I will, Mommy." After she grabbed the crayon, she bent over the paper and concentrated on finishing the animal, the tip of her tongue peeping out of the corner of her mouth.

The sound of Sara's cane hitting the hardwood floor in the hallway preceded her entrance into the kitchen. "I heard laughter and wanted to see what was going on." Slowly she lowered herself in the last chair at the table.

"I took care of the leak. Is there anything else you need fixed?" Caleb leaned toward his toolbox to shut the lid.

"This place is old. There's always something."

"Sara, all you have to do is call." Caleb inhaled a deep breath. "That meat loaf just gets better smelling by the minute."

"You know you can always stay for dinner. We don't stand on ceremony around here." Sara hooked her cane on the back of her chair. "And I agree it smells wonderful."

"I checked it a while ago. It should be ready shortly." Annie turned to her daughter. "Which means you need to put your coloring book and crayons in our room, then wash your hands."

"Do I hafta? I haven't gotten them dirty."

Annie took her hand and showed her the black smudges from the pencil she'd used earlier. "Go, young lady."

Jayden leaped up from the chair and raced from the room.

"Walk. Don't run." Annie waited to hear that

her daughter had slowed down and then said, "Running is her favorite mode of traveling."

"Don't worry about Jayden. It's nice to have a child in the house again. I used to have nieces and nephews who visited all the time before they moved away and got so busy. I enjoyed watching them grow up. To this old lady—" Sara patted her chest "—seeing the world through a child's eyes is like being young again."

"You aren't old."

"Goodness me, Caleb. Have you gone blind? I'm feeling every one of my years right now."

"Age is all up here." Caleb tapped his temple. "By the way, how many years are we talking about?"

"That said, Annie, by one of the young," Sara said, then shifted her sharp gaze to Caleb. "And, young man, it's none of your business. I'm not telling, and you know that." The stern tone belied the gleam dancing in Sara's eyes.

"Ah, but age has nothing to do with how you look at life. And yes, ma'am, I know, but I was trying to help the townspeople." He angled toward Annie. "Her age is a town secret many in Christmas have been trying to figure out."

Sara's laughter filled the kitchen. "It will go with me to my grave."

The humor in Caleb and Sara's exchange touched a much-neglected part of Annie. Working hard as a single mom, trying to make ends meet, had left her without much hope. And now with the threat looming over her and her daughter, she felt weighted down. If she had to disappear as Bryan had insisted, what did she know about doing that? There had been a time in her life when she would have turned to the Lord for help, but maybe the Lord had really forsaken her when she'd lost her direction as a teen.

A few hours later, after a delicious home-cooked meal, Caleb dried the last dish and put it in Sara's cabinet. "I keep forgetting Sara doesn't have the conveniences like a dishwasher for just such an occasion."

"Now she does. At least for the time being." Annie wiped her hands on the tea towel hanging on a hook near the sink. "Me."

"The prettiest dishwasher I've seen." The second he said it he wanted to snatch the words back. His comment produced a pink flush on Annie's cheeks that highlighted her beauty. Caleb tried not to notice. Annie probably wouldn't stick around Christmas long, so why become interested in her? He didn't want his heart broken a second time. Once was enough.

"Thanks." She ran the wet dishcloth around the sink.

Busywork, as though she were nervous. "I just appreciate a home-cooked dinner I don't have to make." Caleb folded the towel and placed it on the counter. "I've got a question for you."

She stopped in mid-rotation, her body tensing. Then as if shaking it off, she completed her turn, throwing a glance over her shoulder.

"Jayden has red hair, but yours is light brown. Was Jayden's father redheaded?" *Great going, Jackson. Why don't you just ask what happened to her marriage? Is the guy still in the picture?*

"Yes." Lowering her eyelashes, she veiled her expression. "I'd better get Jayden to bed. Can I see you out?"

He deserved that. The subject wasn't one she wanted to discuss. Which only piqued his interest. "I can find my way to the front door." He tried to inject humor into his voice, hoping to see Annie's smile.

Instead, she said in a serious tone, "I know Sara's been recovering from a fall. Did she break anything? Was she in the hospital?"

"She fell but didn't break any bones. Her hip is bruised, and she pulled a muscle in her leg. Her doctor forbade her getting up on a ladder anymore. It happened two weeks ago." Caleb passed the front room and gestured toward the eight-foot tree that could be viewed from the street. "Decorating that." At the door he faced Annie, rubbing his hand along the stubble of a day's growth of beard. "Sara tends to want to do everything herself."

"I can understand that."

Caleb stepped closer, taking a whiff of her flowery scent. "The dinner tonight was great."

"Thanks." A dimple appeared in her cheek, enticing him to touch it.

Caleb curled his hands and kept them at his sides. "Good night, Annie. I'll bring Ralph down tomorrow for Jayden to see."

The crisp night air surrounded him as he left Sara's house and strolled toward his smaller home at the end of the block. He'd enjoyed himself a lot tonight, but something wasn't right. He felt it in his gut. During the conversation at dinner Annie had revealed little about herself and her life in Florida, as though she wanted to avoid anything having to do with her past. And really, telling them she was from the Sunshine State wasn't a big secret since her Mustang sported Florida tags.

He would keep an eye on Annie Madison. Even though she was Sara's cousin and his longtime friend hadn't had a problem with an unexpected guest appearing right before Christmas, that didn't mean something wasn't going on. Sara hadn't been expecting her to show up today. This evening Annie had been nervous whenever anything remotely personal came up. Sara hadn't seen Annie in fifteen years. A lot could have changed in that time.

Inserting the key into the lock, he wished he could turn off the cop in him, but it had been drilled into him from his years on the force in Tulsa and now here in Christmas. He would never forgive himself if something happened to Sara.

He was protecting Sara by being vigilant. Or was he really protecting himself? He'd been in a serious relationship in Tulsa, but when he'd asked the woman to marry him and move to Christmas, she'd decided there was no way she could live in a small town, especially one so kitschy. And he'd known better than to date a woman who wasn't a Christian, but he'd thought it might work out. Wrong! And he'd paid for that assumption.

Caleb had been the police chief for two years, ever since he came back to Christmas to take care of his ailing father, who died last year. His death left a hole in Caleb's life. His dad had been his best friend, and he was glad he could help ease the last few years of his life.

He tossed his keys on the table in the foyer and set his toolbox down, then made his way to the den. Ralph lay in front of the fireplace and stood when he saw Caleb. His pet wagged his tail so much that his whole back wiggled in his excitement. Greeting his dog was a great way to end his day.

Tonight while Annie had gone to get Jayden for dinner, Sara had told him she had a gut feeling Annie was in need of a good friend. That the Lord had sent Annie to Sara so she could help the young woman with the adorable child. Caleb wasn't so sure about that. Since her grandniece had moved away last January, Sara had been lonely, even depressed, which definitely could be coloring Sara's perception of Annie.

It was up to him to make sure she wasn't taken advantage of.

Annie rolled over and pounded her fist into the pillow. She should have fallen asleep hours ago, but instead she couldn't shut down her thoughts long enough for sleep to overtake her.

She kept replaying the evening with Caleb. A look he sent her. The touch of his hand. A wink, as though they shared some secret. And then there was his smile. She must have contemplated that for a good thirty minutes. Remembering it bathed her in warmth. She had no business being interested in a man right now. She didn't even know if she would stay in town long after Christmas. After all the commotion of the holidays passed, she needed to decide what she should do next. She had a life back in Crystal Creek she wanted to return to and didn't know if she could.

Frustrated, Annie flipped back the covers and slowly stood, making sure she didn't disturb Jayden sleeping on the other side of the queen-size bed. She paced to the window and pushed the curtain back to peer outside. The blackness of night only reinforced her fear of the dark. She shivered and turned away from the window, letting the drapes fall back into place.

She needed to do something now. Was Bryan alive somehow? How could she find out? Call all the hospitals in that part of Florida? She didn't know their names, but maybe information could help her.

Her gaze fell on her cell, which she'd finally started charging when she'd unpacked earlier. The green light indicated she could use it. She turned it on for the first time since before she'd fled Crystal Creek. When she'd gotten up Saturday, it had been dead, but she hadn't gotten around to charging it before everything changed after Bryan's phone call to her apartment. She'd been too tired to charge it on the road. Annie stiffened. Two messages were on her cell. Afraid of what she might find because few knew her new cell number—one being Bryan—she couldn't keep her hand from trembling.

"Annie, my meeting with my father went badly. He won't acknowledge me. I'm coming to see—" A pause of several seconds then, "I'll call you back. I guess I was going too fast. A cop is behind me and wants me to pull over."

She punched the next message, hoping it was Bryan to explain further, to help her to make some kind of sense of all that was happening. "Annie, you can't run forever. I'll find you, just as I found Bryan."

Listening to the second message from a gruff-voiced man, the same one she'd heard as

Bryan was being beaten, only strengthened the terror that was a constant companion. There was no going back to Crystal Creek.

Chapter Three

The next day at the library computer, Annie stared at the screen, rereading the words of the small article from the Daytona paper: "The body of 28-year-old Bryan Daniels of Daytona was found in a Dumpster behind the McKinney Apartment Complex. The victim was badly beaten and died from a gunshot wound to the stomach. His apartment was later discovered to be ransacked."

He's dead. His place robbed. Tears blurred the words on the screen. Her relationship with Bryan had ended six years ago, but he'd tried to do the right thing concerning Jayden, even if he'd totally messed up his life. How was she going to tell Jayden about Bryan? She had to find a way but make sure her daughter didn't say anything about Bryan to anyone. Maybe when she moved on after the holidays.

Beaten and shot. The facts in the article taunted her. *Oh, Bryan, what have you done? What have you gotten Jayden and me into?*

A noise behind her prompted her to click off the computer before Sara or Jayden found her looking at it. She watched a lady at the counter cross to a cart and place a stack of books on it. Annie scanned the library's large room with rows and rows of shelves and found Jayden sitting cross-legged on the carpet flipping through a book with Sara behind her in a chair peering over her daughter's shoulder.

Shifting back around, she stared at the blank screen. She'd figured after the message last night that Bryan was dead. Reading the news in black and white hammered home that she couldn't go back to Crystal Creek, only fifty miles from Daytona, until she knew what was going on. Had Bryan's visit with his father had anything to do with him being killed? She couldn't go to the cops with what little she knew—not yet, not until she knew whom she could trust. Her life and Jayden's might depend on her silence. She couldn't risk it, especially after Bryan's last message about being pulled over by a cop. That had only been an hour before he called her at her apartment. What had happened in that hour?

What was her next step? Find out more about Bryan's father, Nick Salvador. It had all started with Bryan's visit with him. Who was he? What kind of power did he wield? Where did his money come from? How wealthy was he? Was he capable of killing his own son?

Her head pounded with all the unanswered questions that seemed to demand responses immediately. She rubbed her temples, unable to alleviate the tension.

First, she needed to know if whoever had picked up Bryan's cell and talked to her had found where she lived in Crystal Creek. She dug into her purse and pulled out her cell to call her apartment manager, Trey Johnson.

When he came on the phone, she said, "Trey, this is Annie. I—"

"Where have you been? I've been trying to find you. I don't have your new cell number."

"What?" Annie gripped the cell tighter, again peering around her to make sure no one was nearby. "Why are you looking for me?"

"Your apartment was broken into a few days ago. It was destroyed."

The man found our place in Crystal Creek not long after we'd left!

Her nerveless fingers released her cell, and it dropped to the tile floor making a loud sound in the quiet of the library. Several patrons, including Sara and Jayden, looked at Annie. A flush heated her cheeks as she retrieved her cell and said, "Sorry, I dropped my phone." The rapid thumping of her heartbeat made her voice sound breathless.

"Where are you?"

Light-headed, Annie tried to drag enough air into her lungs, but the room swirled before her. She closed her eyes for a few seconds.

"Annie, are you there?"

"Yes. Do you think anything was taken?" As a friend and manager of the apartment complex, Trey had been in her place several times.

"That's hard to tell, since it was trashed so badly. Even the stuffing in the couch was torn out. Most of what is left isn't salvageable. The police have been here. They aren't saying much, but I haven't heard of any other robberies like yours in town lately."

And Trey would have known. Little crime happened in Crystal Creek—until now.

"When are you coming home? Where are you? I thought you might be dead or something when no one could find you, but your boss told the police you left town for a while. They've been looking for you."

The police, looking for her? The thought escalated her fear and panic even more. "Jayden and I," she began in a voice that quavered, "are okay." *If you don't count having someone hunting us.* "I can't tell you anything else. I'll get back to you later. Thanks, Trey." She clicked off the cell before she told him something that could give her location away. What if the person who had killed Bryan had gotten to Trey?

Don't trust anyone. That included her friends and the police in Crystal Creek.

She turned off the cell, realizing if she was on it long enough they could trace her through the GPS in it. Half the time she didn't have it on because she left it off at work and often forgot to switch it back on. Now all she wanted to do was throw it away, as though the assailant had come through the connection to touch her with evil. She shuddered.

"Mommy, I've got my books. I'm ready to go. Sara wants to take us by the police station to meet Harriet and her blue cat."

"Her cat is at the station?" Annie stuffed the cell into her purse and rose, smiling as Sara made her way to her at a slower gait than Jayden.

"Yeah, isn't that cool? Sara said she's the station mouser."

Fifteen minutes later they entered the police station. The instant Annie saw Caleb, her heartbeat increased as though she'd been given a shot of adrenaline. His gaze latched on to hers and didn't release it.

He disengaged himself from a conversation with an older woman at the back of the station and sauntered toward them, coming around the counter, his eyes sparkling with pleasure. "What brings y'all by here?"

"Jayden said something about wanting to see Harriet's cat, and I told her Samson stays at the station when she's here." Using her cane, Sara moved toward her friend. "Jayden, Samson's usually in his basket near Harriet's desk."

Her daughter trailed behind Sara. The second Jayden saw the cat she stooped next to the large wicker basket and touched the blue-gray animal. Its loud purrs resonated through the room. Jayden grinned and stroked her hand along his back over and over.

"I hope you don't mind us visiting like this. Are you busy?" Annie swiveled toward Caleb.

"I was just taking a break for lunch."

"It's almost two."

"I was busy this morning. We had some vandalism last night." He leaned against the counter, placing his elbow on its top.

"Have you found out who did it?"

"I've narrowed it down to a specific group of teenage boys. Their antics won't last much longer."

"What did they do?"

"Took the ornaments off the town Christmas tree." One corner of his mouth lifted.

"And broke them?"

"Thankfully not. They left them carefully on the ground all around the tree."

Annie chuckled. "Where do kids come up with things like that?"

"The mayor wasn't too happy." Caleb shoved away from the counter. "C'mon and meet Harriet and Samson."

"I was thinking I needed to rescue her from my daughter's endless questions."

"You kidding? Harriet is loving this." He gestured toward the woman with short brown hair and a huge smile on her face.

"Yep, every ornament was on the ground. It took me and some others most of the morning to redecorate the tree. I think Caleb should post guards around it." Harriet peered at Annie as she stopped at the side of the desk near her daughter. "You must be Sara's cousin, Annie."

The woman took Annie's hand and pumped her arm.

"I'll see you tonight," Caleb whispered close to Annie's ear. "I have to pay a visit to one of the boys I think is responsible for the mess in the town square. But first I'll have to deal with the mayor again. He just came in."

Caleb strode toward the middle-aged, stocky man whose dark gaze lit upon Caleb. The town leader's beet-red face attested that his anger was still present. But Caleb's calm demeanor slowly eroded the man's wrath until he let out a deep breath and followed Caleb into his office.

Maybe she could tell Caleb what happened in Florida. Maybe he could help her figure out what was going on and what to do about it.

But as she, Sara and Jayden left to finish their errands, another police officer entered the station. Annie almost ran into him when she opened the door. She quickly sidled away. Although dressed in the same blue uniform as Caleb, this man brought to mind Bryan's warning not to trust the police. As much as she wanted to trust Caleb, she couldn't.

While Sara was reading to Jayden in the living room and the stew was in the Crock-Pot, Annie stepped outside onto the back stoop. Although the temperature was a little above freezing, she relished the crisp air, the perfectly still wind. The sun sank below the tree line, a rosy hue tinting the few clouds in the sky.

The line of fir trees along the back of Sara's property caught her attention. She strode across the yard to get away from the house. She didn't want anyone to overhear her as she made a call. She withdrew her cell from her pocket and called information to find out the police department number in Crystal Creek.

When someone answered, she said to the woman on the other end, "I'm calling about a break-in at my apartment a few days ago."

"Just a moment please."

"Can I help you?" a deep, baritone voice asked a minute later.

"This is Annie Coleman."

Before she could continue, the man said, "We've been looking for you. Where are you?"

"I'm on vacation. Have you found out who broke in?"

"No. Do you have anyone angry at you? Your valuables seemed to still be there, but they were destroyed. Television smashed to pieces, pearl necklace broken and scattered all over the floor. It was more vandalism than a robbery."

Because Bryan's killer was looking for something. "When I return I'll come see you. Thanks." She clicked off quickly, praying she hadn't made a mistake by calling them. She'd kept hoping they might have a clue to who had trashed her apartment. Now she realized that that was wishful thinking.

She turned at the sound of the back door slamming closed and a yelping dog. A big, black mutt bounded toward her with Jayden not far behind. Annie braced herself, but a few feet from her, the dog skidded to a stop.

Her daughter halted next to the animal and threw her arms around him. "Isn't Ralph great? He can even do tricks. Caleb showed me."

At a much more leisurely gait, the police chief approached, again dressed in casual jeans, a blue T-shirt and an open sheepskin coat. "Your daughter wanted to show you Ralph."

"Will you show Mommy how he can roll over?"

"You can get him to by pointing your finger and making a circle in the air," he said with a grin.

Jayden squared her shoulders and inhaled

a deep breath, then drew a circle. Ralph performed the trick while Jayden clapped.

Caleb retrieved a rubber ball from his coat pocket. "He loves to fetch. Do you want to throw the ball for him?"

"Yes!"

As Caleb gave the toy to Jayden, Annie's throat closed at the excitement that brightened her child's face. She ran a few yards, winding up her arm, then lobbed the ball as far as she could. Ralph shot after it. It bounced several times and landed by the back door. Her daughter ran after the dog.

"I'm gonna have to get her a dog. This will cinch it."

"Kids should have a pet. It teaches them responsibility and how to care for something other than themselves."

"Thanks for bringing Ralph over." While Jayden continued to throw the ball for Ralph, Annie started across the yard. "I'd forgotten how quiet this town is. A good quiet. Sara says this is a great place to raise children, that it's so peaceful a lot of people don't lock their doors."

"Yeah, I'm trying to convince them to lock them at least at night, but most of the older folks never have." Caleb paused, his intense gaze skimming her face. "That includes Sara."

"I know. That's when we had the discussion last night about not locking the doors. I did. I told her I couldn't sleep with one eye open." When she did sleep, which had been little lately. "Are you staying for dinner?"

"Of course. I could smell that stew the second your daughter opened the front door. I didn't even have to beg Sara. She asked when I set foot in the living room."

"How did you know it was stew?"

A gleam twinkled in his eyes. "I looked."

Annie stopped at the bottom of the back steps and swung around to watch her daughter. "Jayden, it's time to go in."

Her daughter trudged toward the stoop with the dog bouncing across the yard much like the rubber ball he held in his mouth had.

Five minutes later, Annie entered the living room after checking on the stew in the Crock-Pot and setting the table. Sara sat in her favorite lounge chair while Jayden sprawled on the area rug, busily drawing a picture of Ralph stretched out before the fireplace.

"Caleb, would you be a dear and build a fire?" Sara pulled the edges of her shawl together.

"Sure. I'll need to move some of the items away from the fireplace."

Jayden leaped to her feet. "I'll help." She headed straight for the figure of the baby Jesus, gently lifting it from the manger and cradling it against her as if she were playing with one of her dolls that she'd had to leave in Crystal Creek. "Miss Sara says I can hold him. But I hafta to be *real* careful."

"Are you sure, Sara?" Annie held her breath watching her child handling the eighteen-inch-long figurine, beautifully painted.

"She's fine."

"Here, hon, I'll move the manger for you.". Annie tried not to think about the things they'd left behind in the rented apartment. And according to Trey, all destroyed because someone had searched and trashed her place. Looking for what?

A thoughtful expression slashed her daughter's face. "What's a manger?"

"Child, it's a place where animals eat." Sara rubbed her hands together.

"Why was baby Jesus put in one?"

"Because there was nowhere else for Mary to give birth to Him. The inn—motels were full, so they stayed in a stable." Caleb stacked the logs on the grate then turned the gas on and put a match to it. Flames burst about the wood.

Jayden tilted her head to the side, her eyebrows crunched together. "But isn't Jesus special? He should have a big bed."

"Yeah, Jesus is special, but He didn't mind the manger." Caleb rose and caught Annie's look.

In that moment she knew she had let her daughter down. She might be upset with the Lord because He wasn't answering her prayers, but she should have at least given her child a chance to learn about Him so she would be able to make up her own mind when she was older. At breakfast this morning Sara had talked about going to church on Sunday and had asked them to go.

At one time she had believed that all things were possible through God. She'd been active in her youth group at church, had gone on mission trips. Then she'd made wrong choices when her father had walked out on the family. She'd thrust herself into a murky pattern of self-destruction. She was thankful Jayden's birth stopped that slippery slope downward. But was the Lord mad at her because of her actions?

"Give me about five minutes to get the dinner on the table." Annie averted her gaze and hurried from the room. She wouldn't be using that excuse on Sunday; she needed to take her daughter to church.

In the kitchen she had begun spooning the stew into a serving bowl when Caleb came in.

"Here, let me help." He held the Crock-Pot over the bowl so she could slide the stew into it. "Are you okay?"

"No. I just realized what an injustice I have done to my daughter. I should have taken her to church, but I was angry with God. I still am."

"Why?"

"My life wasn't going the way I thought it should. I prayed and prayed for help, but He didn't answer me. I was basically alone, struggling to pay my bills, raising my daughter with little support…" When she realized what she was telling him, she peered at him to read his expression. Compassion greeted her look.

"What happened to Jayden's dad?"

"He's dead."

"I'm sorry. That makes it tough."

If you only knew.

Caleb set the Crock-Pot on the counter and took her hands. "Look at coming to Christmas as a fresh start. The Lord hasn't forgotten you. He doesn't. He answers in His time, not ours. I'd love for you and Jayden to come to church with me on Sunday."

For a few seconds Annie couldn't concentrate enough to form a coherent reply to his invitation. All her senses were centered on the feel of his hands around hers, the rough texture of his thumb rubbing her skin, his spicy scent wafting to her, putting to shame the aromas of the stew and rolls baking.

"Will you come, Annie?"

She stepped back, grabbing for the pot holders to take the bread out of the oven. "Sara said something about it." She didn't want to care for Caleb. She would be moving on when she could come up with a plan. She needed to return to the library and begin researching how to get lost and stay hidden.

"That's okay. We go to the same one. I'll come by and pick everyone up."

The next afternoon, late, Caleb rang the bell at Sara's. He really didn't have an excuse for visiting, but he was here because he found himself drawn to Annie and Jayden. Since his father's death last year, he'd been going through the motions of living, but something was missing. He wanted a marriage like his parents had.

Whoa. He'd gone from thinking about Annie to thinking about marriage. He still couldn't shake the feeling something was wrong with

Annie. Had someone hurt her? Her deceased husband?

Annie swung the door open. "Hi." Her smile encompassed her whole face, pushing away the vulnerability he'd glimpsed for a few seconds. Now he realized why he was here. He wanted to pump Sara about information concerning Annie. The investigator in him couldn't let go of the fact Annie was harboring pain. He wanted to know what caused it and help.

"What brings you by?"

He pulled his thoughts back to the task at hand. "I came to see Sara."

"Oh, that sounds serious. Is there a problem?"

He schooled his expression into a neutral one, hoping he hadn't given anything away. "No." He should elaborate, but what could he say to Annie? *I've come to find out all I can about you and what made you visit a relative suddenly right before Christmas. One you haven't seen in fifteen years.*

"Were there any more teenage pranks pulled last night?"

"All's calm right now. I issued my warning to the one I think is behind it. Hopefully he heeds it. If not, I may sic the mayor on him," Caleb said with a laugh as he crossed the threshold.

"Is that your secret weapon?"

"No, my art of persuasion is."

Annie closed the door. "Sara is in the living room in her usual place."

"Are you going out?" He noticed she had her coat on, her purse sitting on the table in the foyer.

"Yeah, as soon as Jayden washes up. She had some chocolate and managed to get it all over her face and hands."

Carrying her doll, Jayden bounded down the stairs in her jacket, her hair pulled back in a ponytail that bounced with her lively movement. "Is Ralph here?"

Caleb responded to the little girl's smile with one of his own. "Sorry. I left him at home. I can bring him by later if you want."

"Yes!" Jayden pumped her arm. "We're goin' to the liberrie."

"We've already read the books we got yesterday. We're getting some more. And Sara wanted me to pick up one for her." Annie grabbed her purse. "Ready?"

Jayden hurried across the foyer, snatched up her pile of books and rushed out the door.

Annie shook her head. "I guess she's ready. See you later."

"Bye." He waited until she was gone before proceeding into the living room and taking a seat.

Sara closed the magazine she was reading and placed it in her lap. "I heard you at the door. Did you know Jayden is already reading? She loves books 'bout as much as I do."

"You really have enjoyed having them here, haven't you?"

"I didn't realize how until today. When they first came, I sensed they were lost and looking for something. Well, at least Annie. But so was I. These past few days have brought me back to life. So yes, I've enjoyed them being here. I'm so glad she decided to visit me."

"Did she ever tell you why she suddenly decided to come see you?"

"No, other than she'd always had fond memories of the couple of times she had when she was a child. Especially that last visit, when she and her family came at Christmastime."

"She told me her husband was dead."

"Husband? She said that?" Sara's wrinkles deepened on her forehead.

"Well, not in those words. I asked about Jayden's father."

"Annie has never been married." Sara leaned forward in her chair. "I've been meaning to talk to you about that. I'm concerned about Annie. I think she's in trouble. Earlier today when I asked why she didn't wear a wedding ring, she told me she'd never married the man who fathered Jayden. I'd thought that first day she'd come the name you used to introduce her was her married name, so I didn't say anything. But her real last name is Coleman, at least that was it when she was ten."

Caleb inhaled a deep breath and held it. This was what he'd come for, to find out what was going on with Annie, but he didn't want to hear that she was in trouble. He wanted to be wrong about his gut feeling that something was wrong with her. "Did you say anything about it to her?"

"No. Every time I start asking about what she's been doing she manages to change the subject as quickly as possible. I think my question about the wedding ring threw her, or I'm not sure I would have gotten that much information. Something's not right."

"Are you worried about yourself?" He hated asking that question because his gut told him Annie wasn't someone who would hurt Sara, but he was a cop and Sara was a friend. He *had* to ask.

Sara chuckled. "Absolutely not. I'm a good judge of people, and I see a woman who is hiding something because she's afraid. I catch glimpses of fear in her eyes every once and a while. For instance, yesterday in town a car backfired. She went deathly pale, grabbed Jayden and shielded her. It took her several minutes to calm down, although she tried to hide her fright at the sudden sound. And right after that, Annie was talking on her cell in the library. Her face went pale, and she dropped the phone." Sighing as though relieved she finally shared her concerns, she sat back.

"What do you want me to do?"

"Do some investigating like they do on TV? See if you can find out anything? Most people don't leave home, drive halfway across the country and show up on someone's doorstep they're not even sure is still alive or living where they used to. What made her leave Florida?"

"I'll see what I can find." After hearing what Sara had discovered, his concerns spiraled upward and alarm bells pealed loudly in his mind.

"You said something about bringing Ralph

down this evening. Come for dinner, too. Annie is planning spaghetti. We're eating at six."

"Sold." He came to his feet. "I best be going. See you later."

Outside he paused and drew in a deep breath. What kind of trouble could Annie be in? First thing he would do was drive by the library and get her license plate number and find out where she lived in Florida.

He drove to the library, jotted down her number and then left, not wanting to hang around and have her find him there. He went to his office and ran her tag number. After discovering she lived in Crystal Creek, Florida, he placed a call to the police there.

"This is Caleb Jackson, of the police department in Christmas, Oklahoma. Can I speak to your police chief?"

When the man came on the line, Caleb explained who he was and asked, "Are there any outstanding warrants for a Annie Coleman. She lives in Crystal—"

"I'm familiar with who Annie Coleman is."

Caleb straightened in his chair. "You are? How?"

"Someone broke into her place a few days ago and I'd been trying to locate her ever since.

She finally called me yesterday afternoon and told me she would handle it when she got back to town."

"Do you know who did it?"

"No, but they destroyed just about everything in her apartment. It appears to have happened late Saturday night or the early hours of Sunday morning. Is she in any kind of trouble there in Oklahoma?"

"No, not with the police." When Caleb hung up, he couldn't shake the warning bell going off in his mind. What was Annie into?

He decided to make a call to a friend on the police force in Orlando. Maybe he could dig around and find out what kind of trouble Annie was in? Because everything pointed to a woman on the run. Why?

When Don answered, Caleb took a few minutes to catch up with what was going on with him, then Caleb said, "I have a favor. I need you to find out what you can on Annie Coleman. She lives in Crystal Creek. There was a break-in at her apartment, but from what the police say it sounds like someone that is angry with her or looking for something. They tore her place apart."

"Will do. It may take a few days because I've got a tough case I'm working on, but on my first day off, I'll go to Crystal Creek and do some poking around. Talk with her neighbors. Where she works. I'll even check in with the local police and see if there are any new developments on the break-in."

"Thanks. I owe you." Caleb's hand lingered on the phone after he returned it to its cradle. *Lord, whatever problem Annie is having, let it be one I can help her with.*

Chapter Four

On the computer at the library after searching on the Internet for twenty minutes for information on Nick Salvador, she found an article in a Florida newspaper about him being indicted for murder several years ago. She went through the archives of later issues until she discovered what the verdict in the Salvador trial had been.

She stared at the screen. Terror seized her. He had been acquitted of the murder charge, but the reporter noted that a key witness had never showed up to testify. He'd disappeared. She ran a name search on the witness but didn't find anything pertaining to him. Was he dead? Or living somewhere else?

She pictured something like that happening to her. For a second, panic gripped her. She quickly looked around the library, her heartbeat rapping a mad staccato against her ribs.

"I've got my books," Jayden said, cradling her doll against her chest.

Annie cleared the screen and turned toward her daughter, forcing a smile to her mouth while inside terror still ruled. All she wanted to do was grab her child, hug her tightly and find a way to vanish. Next time she came she would have to research ways to disappear without a trace. There was no way she would risk going back to Crystal Creek now.

"Ready?" Clutching her five books to her chest, Jayden rocked back on her heels.

"Yep, let's go check these out. I need to get back to Miss Sara's and cook dinner." She'd come back tomorrow and do some more searching. She still didn't have any idea what was going on. Maybe the thugs who had trashed her apartment had found whatever they were looking for. What if they weren't looking for an object but for her, because Bryan had called her and she'd overheard some of what happened to him?

On Monday afternoon, Annie grabbed her jacket and hurried into the hall upstairs. She'd promised her daughter she would go for a walk with her today and explore the area. Jayden was taking the idea of being on an adventure seriously, whereas Annie wanted her life back. She'd finished her research today on how to disappear and knew it wouldn't be easy, especially since she had little money. She didn't even have a cell phone anymore. She'd thrown it away after receiving another message from Bryan's killer two days ago. He used Bryan's cell phone again to call her.

His message, "I'm coming to get you," echoed through her thoughts, producing beads of sweat on her forehead and upper lip. She swiped her hand across her face. She couldn't let her daughter see how upset she was. Acting as though nothing was wrong wearied her to the point where she was getting no more than a few hours sleep at night.

Annie descended the staircase, composing her features into a calm countenance for her daughter. Jayden was probably already on the porch waiting, since she wasn't the most patient child. As Annie emerged from the house, she paused. A sudden sense of being watched crawled up her spine, an unpleasant tingling following in its wake.

The last message left on her cell popped into her mind again. She went weak-kneed and clutched the post to steady herself.

Jayden hopped up from the porch swing and skipped to her. "Ready, Mommy? Let's go."

"Sure," she whispered, her throat tight, her mouth dry.

But Annie held her ground for a moment while she scanned up and down the street. There wasn't one car out of place or anyone hanging around. She had been letting her imagination run rampant ever since she listened to her cell phone messages and discovered the type of father Bryan had—one who would go to any lengths to get what he wanted. One who could afford to hire thugs to take care of the messy stuff.

Bryan's killer's messages unnerved her. His taunts indicated he was getting closer. She knew he was doing that to throw her off balance so she would make a mistake. There was no reason to think anyone had found her here in Christmas. She shook off the sensation that someone was out there keeping track of her movements, waiting for the perfect moment to pounce on her.

"C'mon. You promised." Jayden tugged on Annie's hand.

"Fine, but we can't be gone long." When her daughter started to pout, Annie added, "Caleb could still bring Ralph over today. I'm sure you'll want to be here when he does."

Annie followed behind Jayden, who skipped ahead. The feeling she was being watched stuck with Annie all the way around the corner and never ceased, even when she and Jayden started down the road behind Sara's property. What had happened at her apartment had happened in Florida. Not here.

As she strolled near the curb because there was no sidewalk, Annie glanced around at the houses, smaller than those on the street where Sara lived. Fifty feet ahead of Annie, Jayden paused for a second in front of a place and then darted forward. The border of bushes and trees obstructed her view of her daughter.

"Jayden, wait for me." Her shout reverberated down the street.

She hurried her pace, rounding the overgrown hedge in time to see Jayden disappear behind a run-down house that appeared vacant. Her pulse rate increased as her steps did toward the place.

"Jayden, come here."

"Momm*eeee*," her daughter yelled, the sound sending a streak of panic down Annie and propelling her into a flat-out run.

Annie came around the side of the house

and heard her daughter whimpering. Fear draped her in an icy sweat, and she rushed toward the sound, her heartbeat roaring in her ears. Blocked by a large holly bush up against the wooden structure, Annie didn't see where Jayden was until she skirted the shrub and found her daughter down on the ground, one leg stuck in a hole that had been boarded over.

Tears in her eyes, Jayden looked up. "I can't get up. It hurts."

Part of her wanted to wail at her daughter for running ahead of her, but she kept her words inside for later, when she was calmer. "Don't move. Let me see what I can do."

Annie approached Jayden as a large black dog bounded around the corner of the house, barking. Caleb appeared right on his pet's heels. Surprised to see him but relieved to have help, she knelt next to her daughter and began checking out the situation.

"What happened?" Concern on his face, he stooped beside Annie.

"I thought I saw something inside. I was looking in when I fell." Tears rolled down Jayden's cheeks.

"Honey, we'll get you out," Annie said, while she couldn't shake the words her child had uttered. *Something inside? What?* Again the threat in the message played across her mind. No, she couldn't show her panic. She wouldn't give in to what the killer was trying to do. Her call to the police couldn't have been traced to Christmas. And she hadn't left a trail to the town.

"This looks like a hole that the previous owner covered up with some boards. It's been here a while, and most of the wood is rotten. I'll pull Jayden straight up while you try to keep her leg from being scraped any more with the jagged pieces." Standing and leaning over, Caleb put his arms around her child. "Are you ready?"

Jayden nodded.

Annie wedged one hand down between her daughter's leg and the worst broken piece of wood. With the other, she clasped Jayden to help guide the leg straight up. "Ready."

"On the count of three. One. Two. Three." Caleb slowly lifted Annie from the hole.

The action pressed Annie's palm into a sharp, jagged point. Pain flashed up her arm. She bit down and pulled her hand free as soon as her daughter was out. Blood trickled from a cut on her skin.

Ignoring the wound, she angled toward her

daughter on the ground, where Caleb examined the gash visible beneath the torn, ruined cotton pants. She moved to Jayden.

Caleb ripped off a part of her daughter's slacks and tied the strip around her calf to stop the bleeding. "We should have Doc look at this. It might need stitches."

"Stitches!" Jayden's eyes grew round as a full moon.

Ralph licked her child's face, producing a giggle. Jayden threw her arms around the dog's neck and plastered her cheek against his fur.

"Let's get her back to my house. I'll call Doc and let him know you're coming in. Are you ready? I'm gonna carry you, Jayden." Caleb slipped his arms under Jayden and lifted her in one fluid motion.

Balling her throbbing hand, Annie rose. "We need to let Sara know we'll be late. She'll worry."

"Get my cell from my left jacket pocket. Call Sara, then I'll give you Doc's number to dial for me."

She stepped nearer to reach for the phone. When she pulled it out, he started for the front of the house while Annie called Sara and told her what happened and where they were going.

When she hung up, Caleb stopped and spun toward her. "Doc's number is—" His gaze latched on to something over her shoulder. A frown descended.

Annie pivoted and saw the front door of the abandoned house open slightly. "Jayden thought she saw something inside." Annie again felt as though eyes were on her.

His jaw set in a grim line, he handed Jayden to Annie, took his cell, then headed toward the porch. "Wait by the street." He signaled to Ralph to go with Annie, then he cautiously entered the house.

"Mommy, what if the ghost gets him?"

With Ralph next to her, Annie followed his directions and stood at the edge of the property along the road, comforted by the fact a big dog was with her. "Honey, there's no such thing as ghosts. If there was someone in the house, he was very much alive. And while we're on this subject, don't ever run off from me again. Understood?"

"I'm sorry. The house looked haunted."

"It isn't." Annie inched closer to Ralph.

Caleb emerged from the house and crossed the yard to them. The scowl on his face didn't bode well. He'd found something he didn't like.

"Did you see anything?" Jayden asked.

"Nothing to concern you. Let's go get you patched up. That's my priority now."

What did you find? Annie wanted to demand details but clenched her jaw and kept quiet. She would revisit the subject when Jayden wasn't listening.

Caleb started to take her daughter from her when his gaze caught sight of her injury. "You're hurt, too." He paused and took hold of her hand. "You should have said something."

"It's nothing." The feel of his fingers touching her momentarily wiped the dull ache emanating from her wound.

"Doc's gonna have two patients." Caleb took Jayden. "I've already called him, and he'll be at his office."

Two hours later Annie sat in Caleb's car heading back to Sara's with a bandaged hand, a sleepy daughter and a sack of food from the café for dinner. Darkness had fallen over the town, but the Christmas lights lit the night.

Annie peered into the back of the vehicle and saw her daughter nodding off until she slumped over onto the seat. "We didn't get a chance to talk about what was inside the house."

"Someone was using the house to stay in.

I suspect some teens are using it to party. I'll have a word with them tomorrow and put the fear of the law into them."

"Do you think they ran out the front while we were in the backyard?"

"Maybe. I didn't notice if the door was open when I arrived. I was focused on you disappearing around the corner. More likely they forgot to shut it all the way, and the wind blew it open." Caleb pulled up to Sara's and opened his door. "Grab the food, and I'll get Jayden."

Caleb carried her daughter toward Sara's, Jayden slowly waking up and rubbing her eyes. Her wrapped leg testified to her "adventure," one Annie hoped she didn't repeat. The tears in the doctor's office as well as the stitches her daughter had were bad enough, but she didn't know how she was going to pay the bill. Although Doc didn't seem too concerned, she knew the state of her finances wouldn't take many more of these little mishaps, especially if she had to start over somewhere new.

"Sara's probably starved by now. She's used to eating early." Annie took out her key and unlocked the front door then entered.

"I imagine she's more concerned about Jayden than anything."

Before Annie closed the door, Sara stood

in the entrance into the living room. "How's Jayden?" Worry lined her wrinkled face as she moved toward them.

"Miss Sara, I'm okay." Jayden yawned, then stuck her leg out. "See. I got four stitches."

Sara made a production out of examining the bandage. "Doc did a great job fixing you as good as new."

Annie headed for the kitchen. "I'll have dinner on the table in a few minutes. Jayden, go wash up."

Caleb gently set her daughter down, and she limped toward the small bathroom under the staircase.

"Annie, let's have a picnic in the living room." Sara moved toward the room. "I already have a blanket spread on the floor in front of the fireplace. Caleb can fix a fire."

Ten minutes later Annie sat on a large red-and-green plaid blanket eating fried chicken and all the fixings, from biscuits to coleslaw to green beans. With a huge grin, Jayden put her drumstick down on her paper plate, grease smeared around her mouth. Annie handed her a napkin, which her daughter swiped across her face.

As Annie settled next to Caleb, the fire warming her back, he captured her gaze and held it. Her stomach tightened at the gleam that glinted in his eyes. She searched for a safe topic of conversation—one that didn't make her regret her decision to leave after the New Year, all brought on by her fearful feelings and the messages she'd received. She couldn't stay long in any one place. That would give the man time to find her. How she was going to be able to disappear with her daughter was still a question she couldn't really answer.

This town had taught her one thing. If she had to disappear, she needed a place where she could keep to herself. It was much easier that way. There were too many times she wanted to confide in Sara and Caleb. The burden of an unknown enemy out there was taking its toll on her. Especially when she had to seem perfectly fine so as not to arouse any suspicion.

If Nick Salvador or one of his goons were after her, she never wanted to subject the townspeople, especially Caleb and Sara, to someone like him with unsavory connections and accusations of murder in his past. They had all been so kind, accepting her and her daughter.

"How did you know we were on the other block earlier today?" Annie finally asked, although her words held a whispery quality at the intensity flowing from him, all directed at her.

"Sara told me. I just missed you."

"I'm glad you came," Jayden said before Annie could open her mouth. "You saved me."

The admiration in her daughter's eyes probably mirrored her expression, Annie thought. She wasn't good at relationships. The one person she'd really fallen for in the end hadn't been who he'd first appeared to be. She'd thought Bryan was kind, honest and caring, but the only person he'd really cared about was himself. He'd been in Jayden's life when it suited him. And she'd caught him in enough lies while they had dated that when she'd discovered she was pregnant she knew she couldn't marry him. So why was she responding to Caleb? She'd learned her lesson, hadn't she?

"I hope you know now not to go off exploring on your own, especially vacant buildings. They can be dangerous," Caleb said in his police officer voice.

Jayden hung her head. "I won't." She lifted her chin and looked right at Caleb. "I wasn't gonna go in. Promise."

Sara leaned forward and gave Annie her plate. "Remember those marshmallows I got at the store the other day? Let's roast them over the fire. I used to do that as a kid."

Caleb rose then tugged Annie to her feet. "Do you have some metal coat hangers?"

"In the hall closet." Sara waved her hand toward the foyer.

"I'll get them while you get the bag of marshmallows." Caleb picked up the trash Annie couldn't, snagged a mint from a jar on Sara's end table and headed toward the foyer.

After rummaging through the cabinet in the kitchen, Annie found the chewy treat and pulled the bag out. She turned to go back in the living room and nearly collided with Caleb standing behind her.

He hadn't needed to steady her, but his hands clasped her upper arms anyway. The smile deep in his eyes warmed her more than the fire had earlier. Tired of being alone and doing everything herself, she wanted to snuggle into his embrace and feel its protective touch about her.

"How's your hand?" He slid his down her arm to clasp her injured one. Turning it palm up, he peered at it.

"It's quit throbbing," she managed to whisper, although her words came out breathless.

"Good." His gaze stole the rest of her breath. "I worry about you."

The huskiness in his voice constricted her throat, and the intensity in his expression seized her and held her motionless. Worry about her? Bryan certainly hadn't. Somehow he'd dragged her into a mess that might cost her life. "You don't need to. I'm fine." She tried to interject conviction behind that declaration, but Caleb gave her a slow appraising glance.

He combed his fingers through her hair. "If you're in trouble, I can help you."

"In trouble?" Her mind could hardly wrap itself around his words. All she wanted to do was block the world out and just enjoy this man's attention for just a moment in the middle of the nightmare her life had become.

He leaned in, his mouth inches from hers. The scent of peppermint teased her senses. "I take my job seriously."

The whispered words tickled her lips. She closed her eyes, the anticipation of his kiss tapping a fast tempo against her rib cage. When his mouth finally settled over hers, she melted against him, her legs going weak. He wound his arms about her and held her upright while deepening the touch of their lips.

When they parted, he rested his forehead

against hers, and she tried to bring some kind of order to her thoughts. But all she could think about was the dynamite kiss that had been gentle but demanding at the same time. She was in such trouble, and it had nothing to do with Nick Salvador and Bryan's killer. Caleb had the ability to steal her heart. She'd had it crushed once before and because of Bryan might never be able to go home again. That scared her.

The reminder forced her from Caleb's arms. She stepped back against the counter and gripped the edge. "I'll be moving along after the holidays. I'm thinking of heading out west." As far away from Florida as possible.

"Why? If you're looking for a new place to live, what's wrong with settling down in this town?"

Nothing. "Too small." Hard to get lost in. According to what she'd read on the Internet, a big city might be easier to disappear in.

"Oh, I see." Caleb took the marshmallows from her and pivoted toward the hallway. "We better get into the living room before Sara sends out a search party."

Annie stayed for a moment, her grasp on the counter the only thing holding her up. That kiss and her response changed everything, but she couldn't allow it to. She'd fought her battles alone. Nick Salvador could destroy people's lives with his questionable connections, money and hired thugs. She wouldn't do that to Caleb.

By herself, she would keep Jayden and her safe.

By herself, she would find a way to disappear and a place to live.

But as she contemplated the loneliness stretching before her, her thoughts strayed to the kiss that had taken a piece of her heart. She doubted she would get it back. Caleb was the marrying kind of man, one who would protect the people he loved to the end.

Tell him what's going on. Get his help.

She didn't know what was going on. How could she explain it to another?

By herself, she firmed the resolution in her mind and pushed off the counter.

As she entered the living room, she came to a stop just inside and took in that man helping her daughter roast marshmallows over a blazing fire. Jayden's giggles filled the air. Her megawatt grin brightened the room more than the lights. Caleb glanced back at her. His veiled expression didn't reveal anything that had happened in the kitchen, but when she had said

Christmas was too small for her, she'd seen the quickly masked hurt in his eyes.

As Jayden and Caleb prepared the treats for everyone, Sara pushed herself out of the lounge chair and shuffled toward the long table behind the couch. She plucked the ceramic Christmas tree from it and carried it back with her.

"Jayden, I usually decorate every room in the house, but I didn't this year because of my fall." Sara set the tree with colorful painted ornaments down beside Jayden. "Put this in your bedroom. In fact, tomorrow we can drag out the boxes I put away and see what else I have that will add a touch of Christmas to your room."

"Do you have a manger with baby Jesus, Mary and Joseph? I learned about them yesterday in Sunday school class."

"I think I have several in those boxes somewhere."

Jayden clapped. "Yippee. This will be fun."

Sara chuckled. "Christmas is so much better with children around. Too bad you have to work, Caleb, or you could come over and help."

He gave Sara her plate with a roasted marshmallow on it. "I'll stop by at the end of the day, and if there's anything I can hang and put up for you, I will."

A warm, cozy living room with a large Christmas tree in front of the floor-to-ceiling window, garland draped along the fireplace, a blaze in the hearth with the scent of wood permeating the air, snowman figurines everywhere, bright twinkling lights on the tree and intertwined in the wreath hanging over the mantel. She wanted to savor the evening for as long as she could.

"I'm glad you came over tonight." Annie slipped out the front door later and stood with Caleb on the porch. "It'll be fun decorating tomorrow. We didn't get to do much this year at home."

"You didn't want to because you were going to be gone?" He took her hands in his, the touch warm.

Now she realized her mistake. She shouldn't have walked him to the door or come out onto the porch to say good-night. Without Sara or Jayden around, she was afraid Caleb, a police officer who was probably a master at interrogation, would grill her. The whole evening he had asked questions about her life. She'd given him a few tidbits, but not much.

She shrugged. "Why decorate when you

aren't going to be around? We didn't have much anyway."

He pulled her toward the porch swing and sat, tugging her down next to him. "I feel like tonight all I did was talk about myself. You know about my father's death last year. About the reason I left Tulsa. But I didn't tell you the whole story. I was dating a woman seriously in Tulsa and when my father became ill and I knew I needed to return home to help him, I asked her to marry me."

What would it be like married to someone like Caleb who cared about others, was honest and decent? If she had to live her life on the run, she'd never find out. "It's obvious she didn't. What happened?"

"She told me no, said she couldn't live in a place like Christmas. She hated small towns. I was floored. I thought I knew her, and I didn't. It made me question my judgment."

Ah, so when she'd said that this evening, it had brought back memories of the woman in Tulsa. "How do you feel now?" She knew exactly what he had gone through, because she had with Bryan.

"I finally decided the Lord had a hand in it. He had something else in mind for me."

"I wish I had your faith. I did at one time."

In more ways than one. He believed good would triumph over evil in the end. She wasn't so sure, especially with evil lurking out there ready to pounce on her.

With his finger under her chin, he drew her face around so she had to look him straight in the eye. "What happened?"

This she could tell him, and he still wouldn't know what was really going on. Maybe then the questions would stop. "I've made some bad choices, ending with getting involved with Bryan, Jayden's dad. My father leaving sent my mother into a severe depression. She never recovered. Nothing I could do made a difference. She died brokenhearted."

"I'm so sorry, Annie."

Tears crowded her eyes, her throat aching. "I know tragedy happens, but why does it have to?"

"Because we aren't meant to spend eternity here. This is the place where we grow and learn. Sadly that doesn't always happen, when everything goes along merrily with no obstacles to surmount."

"What doesn't break you makes you stronger?"

"Something like that." He used his thumbs to brush away the rivulets of tears flowing from her eyes, then he cupped her face. "Thank you for trusting me with that. You don't know how much it means to me." He bent toward her and kissed her.

In that one gentle kiss he branded her his. From the very beginning he had accepted her, no questions asked. That fact awed her. He hadn't gone behind her back but had waited for her to tell him her story—even if he didn't realize it wasn't the whole story. For the first time in a while she felt hope for the future. Maybe she should say something to him about Bryan's murder and father.

Pulling away, Caleb looked long and hard at her. "I'd better call it a night. See you tomorrow."

As he strolled away, he felt her gaze on him as though she had brushed her hand down his spine. She had trusted him only partially. But she hadn't said a word about the break-in at her apartment in Crystal Creek or the fact all her possessions had been trashed. Why not? Why would that make her flee her home and travel across the country right before Christmas? What else was she keeping from him? He was developing deep feelings for her, and he couldn't allow them to go any further. She wasn't staying in town after the New Year. But mostly even if she was, he had to have total trust.

Chapter Five

Wednesday afternoon, Annie rocked back and forth in the porch swing while Sara took an afternoon nap and Jayden sat on the steps and drew pictures. Bright sunshine and warm temperatures made the day beautiful, promising. But inside Annie couldn't unwind. Her stomach remained in a tight knot, as though a nest of vipers lay curled in a lump, waiting to strike and inject her with their poison.

With a glance at her watch, she rose. "Honey, I have to put the clothes into the dryer. I'll be right back."

She hurried into the laundry room and transferred the wash to the dryer. What little clothes they'd brought with them she'd cleaned several times since they'd arrived last week. She'd never had a lot of clothing, but she'd had to leave at least half behind in Crystal Creek. In that moment, the thought of having to start over in a new place—get a job somehow, find a cheap place to live—overwhelmed her. She slammed the dryer door closed and leaned into the appliance to steady herself.

Why, Lord? Why me?

No answer came to mind. She couldn't give in to self-pity. It wouldn't change her situation or produce a solution. She would survive and protect Jayden. She had no other choice.

She pushed off the dryer and scrubbed her hands down her face as though that could miraculously wipe any fear from her expression. She made her way to the foyer, stopping halfway across it when Jayden came into the house, carrying a wrapped present.

"Where did you get that?" Annie covered the few feet to her daughter.

Jayden held it up to her. "He gave it to me and told me to tell you it was from a secret Santa."

"Caleb?" Annie took the gift from her.

"No." Jayden shook her head several times to emphasize the point. "A stranger. I promise I didn't say anything to him. You told me never to talk to a stranger."

Chills encased Annie. "What did he look like?"

"Big."

"Anything else?"

"He wasn't Santa. He had dark hair. He came in a car, not a sled."

"What color was the car?"

"Black and big."

He could have taken Jayden. The rapid beating of her heart thundered in her ears. "Thanks, honey. Let's get your stuff and come inside." Somehow she'd managed to keep her voice level, the panic from sounding in it. But inside it raged, squeezing around her chest until she could hardly breathe.

When she stepped onto the porch again, Annie surveyed the street. As it was two days before, nothing was out of place—no strangers, no cars that shouldn't be. She'd only been gone five minutes.

After Jayden collected her pad, Annie hurried her inside and locked the door. "Why don't you go draw in our room? I'll be up there in a few minutes."

As her daughter bounded up the stairs, Annie peered out the small window in the foyer. Still nothing. She strode to the kitchen, made sure the back door was locked, then looked outside the window there. No sinister man lurking around the yard.

She sat at the table and slowly opened the package. Her hands quaked so badly she fumbled, taking twice as long as she should have. Inside the box lay a 5x7 photo of Bryan, Jayden and her he'd taken last summer. Jayden had a smaller version in her treasure chest she'd brought with her, while Bryan had framed a 5x7 picture and put it by his bedside. At least that was what he'd told her.

On the glossy page a big X was marked through Bryan. The words, You're next, were written across her image. She dropped the photo, so cold she couldn't contain her trembling. Rubbing her hands up and down her arms, she tried to erase the goose bumps from them, to warm herself. She couldn't.

Bryan's killer is here.

Caleb pushed to his feet and scooted his desk chair back. When he exited his office, he peered at the wall clock and noted the time. 2:00 p.m. He needed to grab something to eat and try to straighten out what was going on in his town. Heading toward the door to the station, he went over his earlier interview with several of the teens he'd thought had used the vacant house behind Sara to party in. None of them had, according to their protests. The three boys had seemed genuinely surprised when he had questioned them. If they were telling the truth, then who had used the house? He'd sent Jeremy, one of his police officers, over to see if he could get any fingerprints. He hadn't bothered yesterday, but now he'd give it a try, although the chances of finding the culprit's prints were slim.

Looking up and down North Pole Boulevard, Caleb started across the street for the café. Suddenly he heard the shriek of tires and peered to his left. A black SUV with dark tinted windows came barreling around the corner and headed right toward him. He dove between two parked vehicles on the other side of the street as the car whizzed by him. Scrambling to his feet, he tried to make out the tag number. Mud covered the license plate.

His palms stinging, he flipped open his cell and made a call to Tyler, another officer on patrol. He gave him what information he could on the vehicle and had him keep an eye out for it. If he hadn't reacted quickly, he could have really been hurt. Lunch forgotten, Caleb limped back across the street to the station to get his keys, which he'd overlooked on his desk. He would do his own patrolling, too.

* * *

Annie rushed into the bedroom she shared with Jayden and went to the closet, pulling out their suitcases then stuffing the still wet clothes from the dryer into one of them.

Jayden looked up from drawing at the small round table. "Are we going someplace?"

"Yes, a new adventure. C'mon. Start packing your stuff."

"I don't wanna leave." Jayden threw down her crayon.

"We're playing a game to see how fast we can get everything in the car. I think we can in ten minutes. What do you think?"

Jayden's eyes brightened. "Maybe. What do we get if we win?" She leaped up from the chair and raced toward the dresser to get her clothes.

To stay alive. "It's a surprise," Annie said, frantically trying to think of anything to say to get her daughter to cooperate. She wanted to be gone before Sara woke up from her nap. She didn't want to answer any questions.

All she knew was she needed to leave Christmas. She couldn't stay. He was here! Her heart hammered so quickly the room spun. She paused and inhaled a fortifying breath. *I can't fall apart. I can't fall apart.*

I can do all things through Christ, who strengthens me. The verse infused itself into her mind, and a calmness descended.

Ten minutes later, Annie stopped at the back door and searched the yard and driveway. Empty. She released a breath through pursed lips. She and Jayden left the house and covered the distance to her car parked in front of the detached garage. After stuffing their suitcases into the trunk, she got into the front and inserted her key into the ignition. When she turned it, nothing happened. She tried again.

Dead. As dead as she was going to be if she stayed.

Desperation drove her to try yet a third time. Nothing. She pounded her fist on the dashboard. That was when she saw the piece of paper that had slipped down near the windshield.

She read it. *You can't hide. You're mine anytime I want.*

"Mommy, what's wrong?

What should I do?

Tell Caleb. Get help.

That calmness still clung to her. She turned to Jayden and smiled, although the effort to maintain it made her lips quiver. "Let's see, how long did it take?" She checked her watch. "We did it in eleven minutes."

"We lost?"

"No, we didn't. And I think there's some ice cream in the freezer that has your name on it."

"Chocolate."

"Yep."

Jayden leaped from the car and raced for the back door. Annie exited and popped the trunk, taking their suitcases and following her daughter inside. Trying desperately to remain calm for Jayden, she fixed her daughter a large bowl of ice cream and then went to the hall phone and dialed Caleb at the police station.

"Annie, it's nice to hear from you after the bad day I've had."

"What happened?" She fought to keep her voice from wavering but her hands shook.

"A few minutes ago I almost got run over right outside the police station."

Annie straightened. On purpose? "Did you catch the person?"

"No, but I'm leaving and going out to look. What do you need?"

She couldn't tell him over the phone. "I hope you'll stop by later. Let me know what happens."

"I'll see you this evening and we'll talk."

She started to go back into the kitchen when the phone rang. She snatched it up, not wanting to disturb Sara. "Hello."

"Hi, Annie. Did you get my little present? I know it's a little early for Christmas, but I didn't want you to think I'd forgotten you," the deep, gruff voice of her tormentor said.

She shuddered at the implication of his words. "What do you want?"

"You know. And just so you don't get any ideas about telling your boyfriend about what's going on, I wanted you to know I'll actually kill him the next time. Today was your one warning."

"You tried to run him down."

"It was so much fun. Or maybe he's not enough of an incentive to keep quiet. Maybe instead, I'll take Jayden. She's a pretty little girl. Not very talkative, though."

"You wouldn't."

His cackle right before he hung up was her answer. With the receiver in hand, Annie sank to the floor and leaned her head back against the wall. She couldn't leave. And she couldn't tell Caleb.

Thursday night, Caleb turned off the ignition to his police cruiser in the church parking lot and laid his head against the steering wheel. The last few days had been hectic, especially after nearly being run over yesterday. His body still protested his contact with the asphalt surface of the street.

This morning the black SUV had been found outside of town, ditched in a field. It had been stolen the day before and all prints had been wiped clean. On the other case, Jeremy had found some usable fingerprints in the vacant house and was running them for a match. But that could take time.

He didn't like everything that was happening in Christmas lately. He had someone he was falling for obviously in trouble and not saying anything to him. Last night he'd tried again to get her to talk, but she hadn't. He had someone who had deliberately headed right toward him on the street. And he had someone, maybe more than one, using the vacant house without the knowledge of the owners, who he'd contacted yesterday.

The ringing of his cell cut into his thoughts. "Jackson here."

"I've got something else for you, which may or may not be connected to your Annie Coleman," his friend Don from the Orlando Police said.

Caleb sat up straight, peering toward the doors to the church. "What?"

"Her landlord is in the hospital in a coma. Someone beat him up bad. Nearly killed him."

"When?"

"Middle of last week."

"Any suspects?"

"No. I also discovered her daughter's father was found dead—beaten up and shot in the stomach."

Caleb's gut constricted into a hard ball. "No suspects?"

"You got it. This doesn't bode well for your Annie."

My Annie. The woman who wouldn't say a word to him about what was going on. One way or another he would get to the bottom of this tonight. He was through waiting for her to tell him. "If you hear anything else, call."

He slipped from the front seat and crossed the parking lot to find his Annie.

"I was gonna borrow Harriet's car to go get the box of garland. I'm glad you showed up," Annie said as she walked toward Caleb's vehicle parked in the church lot, not five minutes after he arrived. "You look tired."

"Just working hard." He took her hand, a

frown creasing his forehead. "You are shaking. Are you okay?"

No, my life is in shambles. I don't know what to do about the man who murdered Bryan. He could be anywhere. Watching. Waiting. But if I say anything, he'll hurt someone I care about. "Too much caffeine."

"You look like you're not getting much sleep."

"I never sleep well in a new place." She slipped into the front passenger seat. When Caleb had come into the rec hall, the grim look on his face concerned her. Had the killer tried something else with him? "Did you find out anything about who tried to run you over?"

"No," he clipped out and started the engine, then backed out of the parking space. "What happened to your car? Why did you come with Harriet this evening?"

Ah, the questions again. She delayed answering as long as she could. "I went to try it and it was dead. I had it towed this morning to the garage. They haven't told me what's wrong yet. It's ten years old."

He turned down Bethlehem. "We need to talk."

"We can after the greening of the church. I don't want to leave Jayden too long with Harriet. She'll talk the woman's ear off about her cat. Besides, with all those kids running around, they need all the adults they have to get the job done before the party Saturday night."

"Fine. I'll bring you and Jayden home this evening instead of Harriet. You get the box of garland Sara called about and I'll get the step-ladder they need."

She opened the door. If she kept busy, maybe she could get through this evening at church and not fall apart in front of everyone. "It shouldn't take long, but I want to check on Sara. I think she overdid it yesterday and her hip is giving her trouble."

"I'll grab my ladder and be back here."

Annie jogged to the porch and dug into her jeans pocket for the house key. When she entered, the glow from the Christmas lights Sara liked to leave on would give her enough illumination to see her way toward the small storage room off the kitchen. Sara must have gone to bed right after she called her at the church.

As Annie passed the living room, she froze. Inside it, Sara was tied up in her chair with a gag over her mouth, her eyes wide with fright.

Chapter Six

Annie whirled toward the front door and took a couple of steps when someone slammed into her. His beefy arms snaked around her, trapping her against his large body.

"Well, well, you came quick, Annie."

The sound of the intruder's voice generated a rush of memories. Of holding the phone listening to Bryan being beaten up. The noise when the gun went off. The same deep, gruff voice taunting Bryan, demanding answers. His threat to find her. To kill Caleb or take her daughter.

Panic seized her in a stranglehold, her body washing in hot and cold flashes almost simultaneously.

He killed Bryan. And he was here for her.

The assailant held her up off the floor, the

upper part of her stuck to him like glue. But her legs were free. She swung one back and whacked him in the shin. He groaned. She struck him again, one of her shoes flying off. That didn't stop her. She kept hammering at him.

He groaned and muttered a few words that fired her determination to get away. "What did Bryan give you? Where is it?"

"I don't know what you're talking about," she screamed as she swung back her foot with her slip-on shoe to hit him again. Not expecting the sudden release when he dropped her, she crumpled to the floor.

"I'll get it from you one way or another. We've looked everywhere else. We know you have it." He blasted her with his fury, towering over her. "Remember what happened to Bryan. I can do the same to her and you," he said, indicating Sara in the chair.

"I don't know what you're talking about." She poured all her confusion into her voice and expression. She couldn't give the man something she didn't have. *Lord, help.*

Hauling her to her feet, he pushed his face into hers, the scent of garlic and onions assaulting her. "Bryan gave you something to keep for him. Where is it?"

She screamed again.

He slapped her, sending her head reeling to the side. Her ears rang with the sound of his hand striking her cheek, reminding her of what he'd done to Bryan. Cold fury and fear tangled together, vying for dominance.

"If you scream again, you'll regret it." He pulled a knife out of his pocket then put it back. "Where are your things?"

"Upstairs." She balled her hands in preparation to punch him in his belly and then run.

But before she could, he hefted her over his shoulder and started for the stairs. "Show me."

The air swooshed from her lungs as her stomach connected with his shoulder. The blood rushed to her brain. She managed to kick off her other shoe while trying to hit him.

Where's Caleb?

As the intruder climbed the steps, her cheek impacted with his back with each jostling move. The farther away she was to the shoe at the bottom the more her fear grew that Caleb wouldn't reach her in time. She had to do something. She fisted her hands and pummeled his back.

On the second level he unceremoniously set her down, and she grabbed for the banister to steady herself.

"Which room?"

"That one." With a shaky hand, she pointed to her bedroom where she and Jayden were staying.

He gripped her arm and yanked her down the hall. She tugged in the opposite direction, dragging her feet. The assailant had killed once before, and she wasn't a fool who thought she would make it out of this alive if she gave him what he wanted.

Caleb sat in his car out in front of Sara's listening to the radio with the stepladder lying across the backseat. For the fifth time he checked the clock on the dashboard.

Where's Annie? She should be out here by now.

He shoved out of his vehicle and headed for the house. On the porch he found the front door ajar and pushed it open. He scanned the foyer. His gaze riveted to one of Annie's shoes lying on its side near the stairs. Then he caught sight of the other one in the entrance into the dining room. Alarm bolted through him. Still dressed in his uniform, he drew his gun.

As he eased toward the living room, warning bells clanged full force in his mind. When

he peeked inside, he spied Sara tied up. He rushed to her, removing the gag.

"Where's Annie?" Caleb started untying her.

"A man took her upstairs. He's looking for something. Go. I'm okay."

He quickly undid the last knot, saying. "Call the station," then moved out into the foyer. He quickened his pace and climbed the stairs two at a time.

The assailant tossed Annie on the bed. He withdrew the switchblade from his pocket again, the movement exposing the gun strapped to his belt under his jacket. Her panic surged to a level that threatened to incapacitate her.

"I don't have time for games. Where is it?"

While his gaze swept the room, she inched toward the side away from Bryan's killer.

His steely look fell on her, his forehead puckered. "I'd hate to cut that pretty little face. Move again and I will. Where is it?" He shouted the last sentence.

"I've been trying to tell you I don't know what you're talking about. Bryan hasn't given me anything to keep for him. What is it you're looking for?"

"You know. I have a way of loosening the

tongue." He caressed the length of his knife as though he were stroking a woman he loved.

Every muscle locked in place. *Where's Caleb?*

Bryan's killer knelt on one knee on the bed, his dark eyes pinning her down.

Terror crammed her throat. She crawled to the side and back, trying to get away from him.

Plastered against the wall outside the bedroom, through the crack in the open door Caleb saw the man kneel on the bed near Annie, her eyes wide, her face as white as the coverlet she was on. He shifted to pivot into the entrance and aim his gun.

Protect Annie, Lord.

With a calming breath, Caleb swung into the entrance and pointed his weapon at the man's chest. "Police. Drop the knife, now!"

The intruder hesitated, his gaze flying toward the door.

"Don't make me use this," Caleb said as Annie scrambled from the bed, out of reach of the man.

The clunk of the knife as it hit the hardwood floor echoed through the room.

"You're okay?" Caleb asked Annie without taking his eyes off the intruder.

"Yes." She hurried toward him. "He has a gun in a holster on his belt."

Her brave front that vied with her quavering voice made him want to hold her and reassure her he wouldn't let anything happen to her. But he couldn't until he took care of the man. "I untied Sara. Make sure she's okay."

"Will you be okay alone?" Annie skirted around Caleb.

His chuckle eased some of his tension. "I think I can manage."

As soon as Annie made her way down the stairs, Caleb said to the intruder, "Kick the knife under the bed, then lie facedown on the floor in the middle of the room, arms outstretched."

The second the assailant complied, Caleb approached him, his gun at all times pointed at the man's back. After patting him down and removing his Glock, Caleb withdrew his cuffs and snapped them on the suspect and then jerked him upright. It took all his willpower to keep from slamming the man a few times up against the wall.

As he descended to the first floor with his suspect, Caleb heard Annie in the living room talking with Sara. Her voice still shook, but with each word it grew stronger. The thought of what this man in front of him could have done to Annie twisted his gut in a hard knot.

Later that night, when everyone had left and Jayden and Sara went to bed, Annie came down the stairs, the soft glow from the fireplace and the lights on the Christmas tree in the front window drawing her toward the living room and Caleb, who was waiting for her. When she entered, she found him poking the blaze, sparks flying up the chimney.

Putting the poker up, Caleb rotated toward her. For a long moment, he didn't say a word, but his visual tether roped her to him. Words fled her mind.

Slowly the corners of his mouth inched up. "Is Jayden tucked in?"

"When her head hit the pillow, she was almost instantly asleep. I wish I could go to sleep that fast." Exhaustion cleaved to her. The past few hours had been hectic, but she was happy to be alive. She could have ended up dead, like Bryan.

"Sara?"

"She's fine. Told me she was made from sturdy stock." She wished she could say the same about herself. She clasped her hands together to still their quivering.

"That man acted like he knew you. What was he after? He isn't saying anything except he wants a lawyer." His perceptive gaze held her again.

Tell him everything, not just part of it. You can't do this alone anymore, and it's not over. What if the assailant's acting on Nick Salvador's orders?

Caleb's forefinger whispered a path across her face, along her cheekbone. "I can see your worries in your gaze. He can't hurt you anymore."

She closed her eyes. "I know I'm an open book. I wish I wasn't."

"I like you the way you are."

His words weaved their way through her mind, tantalizing her with the idea she could put down roots in Christmas, be a part of the town, be a part of Caleb's life. She lifted her eyelids and looked at him. The warm expression, as if she were special to him, only added fuel to that fantasy.

"Annie, you can trust me. I care for you and Jayden. You can't do everything alone. We all need others." He took her hand and led her toward the couch. "What's going on? I can help you."

She couldn't resist his enticement. He was

offering her something she hadn't had in a long time: someone to confide in. *Did You lead me to Christmas for this, Lord? Is Caleb Your answer to my prayers for help, for a solution to my problem?*

He sat so close his leg pressed against hers. He slipped his arm along the back of the couch, cocooning her in the shelter of his embrace, loose but protective. "I see a look in your eye that tells me you've been hurt. You're still hurting and it goes beyond what you told me a few days ago. It has something to do with the man I have in my jail."

Dropping her gaze to her lap, her hands twisting together, she nodded, the pain of the past swelling in her chest. "And with Jayden's father."

"Tell me about him. You said he was dead. When?"

She sucked in a fortifying breath. "He died twelve days ago."

"I'm sorry, Annie."

The words she needed to say lodged in her throat. She was so tired of holding everything inside. "I wasn't ever married to him. In fact, he didn't live in the town I lived in but Daytona. I saw him occasionally because of Jayden." Trying to prepare herself for a disappointed look in Caleb's eyes, she glanced toward him. What she saw stunned her. There was no condemnation, only sympathy. "We met in college. I fell head over heels in love. Until I got to know the real Bryan. He was exciting, charming and in the end totally focused on himself. He partied too much. He drank too much. He even went to jail for a DUI. He asked me to marry him, but I couldn't, not even when I found out that I was pregnant. It would have been a marriage doomed from the beginning. He didn't have much money, so he didn't help much with raising Jayden except to sweep into her life every once in a while, give her presents, then sweep back out."

"I'm sorry you had to go through that alone. I don't understand a man chucking his responsibilities, especially to his own daughter."

"I learned to take care of things myself."

"But you don't have to. I'd like to help. Sara cares about you, too."

She wouldn't think of what his words implied—that he cared about her possibly more than a friend. "You don't really know me."

"I know a woman who loves her daughter and has done a great job raising her. I know a woman who's been wonderful with Sara, giving her a reason to look forward again to

Christmas. You don't have to worry about going it alone anymore. You don't have to leave town when your car is fixed."

"I'm used to going it alone. That's not what I'm worried about." She collapsed back against the cushion, tired of holding herself so tense that her muscles ached. "Bryan got into something bad and somehow pulled me into it. I got a call from him the day he was killed—murdered."

"Murdered?" Caleb pulled her into the crook of his arm as though to prove to her she wasn't alone, that he was right there with her.

"I wasn't sure exactly—I'm still not—what was happening when he called. But I read later he was found beaten and shot. I heard it happen, and the man you have in jail is the one who killed Bryan, although I didn't see him do it."

Caleb tensed. "What happened?"

"The killer interrupted the call to finish the deed. Bryan called me to warn me not to trust anyone and to run and hide." She turned toward Caleb. "And before you ask me why, I have to tell you I don't know the reason. All I know is that he was going to finally pay his father a visit. The father he didn't know he had until after his mother died last month."

"So that man is Bryan's father?"

"No, but I think his father sent that man after Bryan. After what I learned about who his father is, it's definitely a possibility. But then again, why would the man do that to his own son, even if he didn't know about him? I know that Bryan thought this was the answer to all his financial woes, but still…" She let her voice fade into silence, still perplexed by the whole situation.

"Who's his father?"

"Nick Salvador, a man who lives in Tampa and is basically a wealthy criminal from all I can learn. The last thing I knew, Bryan was in Tampa to meet him."

"So he got mixed up with the wrong guy? I've seen that before, and I've even seen a father kill his son, but you're right that there are definitely questions that need answers."

"From what I could tell, the person with Bryan in the end wasn't his father. The little I heard didn't indicate that at all. The reason I didn't go to the police is that Bryan warned me not to even trust them. And the last message he left me on my cell phone was he'd left his father's disappointed. The meeting went badly with Nick Salvador. Bryan started to tell me something else when he was pulled over by a cop. Then not an hour later Bryan called me at home. He was running for his life. That's when I heard him being killed."

Caleb sucked in a deep breath, his face paling. "So somehow Bryan thought the police might be involved?"

"That's why I didn't know where to turn. When the man called me, I panicked and fled Crystal Creek. After about a day on the road, I decided to come here and hide. Sara was my mother's second cousin. When we came to Christmas all those years ago, it was really to see Sara's mother. My mother and hers were close at one time. I just ended up over here a lot because I loved Sara's house. Great places to hide. That's what made me think of Sara and Christmas." Palms sweaty, she rubbed them on her jeans. "I know I can't stay long. I don't want to in any place until I figure out what's going on."

"Why didn't you tell me?"

"Because the man you caught tonight threatened to kill you. He's the one who tried to run you down. He was making a point to me that anyone I cared about could be hurt if I said anything to you."

"No more running, Annie. It ends here. I'll protect you." Anger laced his voice, the muscles in his arms still bunched. "If Nick Salvador is behind this, we'll deal with it on *my* turf."

She inhaled a soothing breath, and yet it did nothing to calm her.

"And until we get to the bottom of this whole situation, I'll be with you, or one of my men will." He patted the couch cushion next to him. "I'm a light sleeper. This will serve nicely as a bed. I'm staying here at night. Sara would be the first one to agree to that."

"I can't ask you to do that."

"You aren't. I'm insisting, as the police chief of Christmas. There won't be a repeat of this evening." Caleb brushed his hand through her hair, then leaned down and kissed the tip of her nose, saying, "You're safe in my town." Then he proceeded to graze his lips over each corner of her mouth.

The sensations bombarding her from all sides made it difficult to think straight. All she managed was to nod her head. Everything else took too much thought.

After sampling her lips in a deep kiss, he framed her face. "Let's go out together tomorrow night to take your mind off all that's happened."

"A date?" She hadn't been on one since Bryan,

and look what happened there. Wariness inched into her thoughts.

He chuckled. "Yes, a date. How about it?"

"Yes," she whispered, right before he kissed her again.

Chapter Seven

Sitting at his desk on Friday, Caleb scrubbed his hands down his face. He hadn't slept at all the night before. Sara's couch had been comfortable enough, but his mind kept going over and over all the facts and questions concerning Annie and what had happened the evening before. Bruce Downey, the suspect, still hadn't said a word, and from what Caleb understood, a lawyer was arriving later today. An expensive, high-powered one from Oklahoma City.

What bothered him the most was that Downey was an ex-policeman for the Tampa Police Department. That ate at his sense of fair play. Had he stopped Bryan and pretended to still be a cop? It appeared Bryan knew his attacker had a connection to the police.

A match for a fingerprint found at the vacant house came back a little while ago. It was Downey's. How long had he been in town watching Annie? Waiting for his chance to get her alone.

He flinched at the sudden ringing of the phone cutting into the silence. Snatching it up, he said, "Jackson here."

"I got some more information for you," Don said.

Caleb had called his friend in Florida first thing when he'd arrived at the station this morning. "Shoot."

"Nick Salvador has disappeared. No one has seen him for the past day. Someone thought he might be on vacation in Mexico."

"You think he's fled the country?"

"No, I don't think anyone knows where he is. He's bad news. I'm warning you to keep your guard up. Someone I know on the Tampa police force said it's been rumored that Downey went to work for Salvador. Downey was basically kicked off the force three years ago."

"Thanks. If you hear anything else, I'd appreciate a call. I feel like I'm flying in the dark."

"I'd hate to see you crash. I'll call if I hear anything."

After Caleb hung up, he stared at his phone

and decided to call Tyler, the police officer watching Annie. "Everything okay?"

"Quiet. Well, not exactly quiet. Jayden is dancing to some Christmas music in the living room and Sara is keeping time to the song."

"Where's Annie?"

"Fixing us lunch. She's serving us leftover homemade chicken pot pie."

Remembering when she served it the first time, Caleb licked his lips, his stomach churning his hunger. "I'll be there in a few hours. The man who might be behind what happened last night has disappeared in Florida. Don't let down your guard."

As soon as Caleb finished with Tyler, the questions returned to plague him. What had Downey been looking for? The only thing that Bryan had given Annie lately was the family Bible and he'd checked that out. Nothing.

Christmas lights strung everywhere illuminated the downtown area in a glittering fairy-tale setting. The last burst of fireworks Friday night sprayed across the dark sky, a multicolored display that stole Annie's breath.

"You guys go all out here in Christmas." Annie made another visual sweep of the square at the south end of the main thoroughfare. All it needed was a blanket of snow to complete the effect of a twinkling winter wonderland. "First a great meal, and now this light celebration."

"Kinda goes with what we're doing this evening, celebrating." Caleb clasped her hand and began walking toward his car. "Tomorrow is our last fireworks display. Let's bring Sara and Jayden down here after the Christmas party at church. I'm sure they're watching from the house, but it's better from the town square."

"Sounds nice." *Making plans for the future.* She wanted to be able to do that, but after all that had happened in the past few weeks, she realized how quickly her life could change.

At his vehicle he opened the door for her. "I'm hoping Downey decides to talk, but even if he doesn't, he'll be going away for a long time with what we have here. And I talked to the FBI late this afternoon about Nick Salvador. They'll be sending someone down from Oklahoma City tomorrow to talk to you and Downey. They are interested in what happened. Nick Salvador has been on their radar for years." He stepped closer, cupping one cheek. "Put your worries in the hands of the Lord. Between Him and me, you'll be all right."

"I'm trying. It isn't always easy. I want to control every aspect of my life so I don't have any more surprises like what happened with Bryan."

"But we aren't really in control. God is and He's perfect for the job. He knows the future. We don't."

She gave him a smile. "Thursday night I asked for help, and He sent me you."

He roped her against him. "I'm glad I could help. I want to be there for you."

A parishioner Annie met at church passed by on the sidewalk and greeted them. Caleb backed away from Annie. A red tinge, highlighted by the streetlamp a few yards away, colored Caleb's cheeks.

"I guess we'd better go to Sara's." Caleb gripped the doorframe.

"We can finish our...talk there."

Annie slipped into the passenger seat, the heat from her own blush warming her face. She hadn't flirted in years, and yet that was what she'd been doing. As she watched him round the front of the car, she realized she was falling in love with him. She didn't know if their relationship was possible, because if she had to leave Christmas to protect Jayden she would. After Christmas she needed to reassess her situation concerning Nick Salvador.

Behind the steering wheel, Caleb started the car and pulled out of the parking space along the main street. He scanned the area as he drove by.

"You won't be able to keep protecting us indefinitely," Annie finally said, disturbing the comfortable silence between them.

"We'll deal with that when we have to. Let's see what the FBI have to say about the situation. They may be able to locate Salvador and keep an eye on him."

"If you say so."

"I'm not gonna let Salvador win." He pulled into Sara's driveway.

When Caleb climbed from his vehicle, Annie started to open her door but stopped. He liked to do that, and she was learning to let him. She was so used to opening her own door that she had to work to curb the impulse.

On the walk to the porch she relished the crispness in the night with the scent of burning wood from the neighbor's fireplace lacing the air. With Caleb's arm around her, she mounted the steps. Sara had left the outside light off, but the Christmas ones all around them lit the dark shadows.

At the top of the stairs she turned toward him, not wanting the evening to come to an end yet. "I can fix some hot chocolate, if you want."

He framed her face, his amiable gaze fixed on her. "I'd better try to get some sleep tonight. Tomorrow will be another full day, especially with the FBI here." He moved closer, his arms winding about her. "Are you and Jayden gonna stay after Christmas?"

"It's a possibility." One she wanted to make happen with all her heart. Caleb made her feel cherished. No one had made her feel that way, not even Bryan when they had been dating. She didn't want to give that up, but so much depended on what Nick Salvador did. Even if she was falling in love with Caleb, her daughter had to come first, and she couldn't live her life with him always having to protect her. She would have to have another solution—even if that meant somehow disappearing somewhere else.

"I'll just have to keep working on you. I can be very determined when I need to be."

"If I stay, I'll have to find a job soon. I can't continue to live at Sara's. I don't want to outstay my welcome."

"In the few weeks you and your daughter

have been in Christmas, Sara has become her old self again. She'd probably have something to say about that."

"Maybe I could find a job and rent a room from her. Still be here and even help her."

He nestled her against him. "I like how you think. What kind of work have you done?"

"I went to college for a year but had to leave when Jayden was born. I've recently been an office manager of a roofing company in Crystal Creek."

"I'll see what I hear through the grapevine." He bent closer. "But you've given me inspiration to see what I can find."

His last words whispered across her lips, tickling them, right before he touched his mouth to hers, quickly lengthening the kiss. In that moment Annie knew she wasn't just falling in love with Caleb but that she was in love with him. Her heart soared with the thought, only to plummet a few seconds later when she realized the implication. She might have to walk away from the best thing that had happened to her besides the birth of her daughter.

When they parted, he took her hand and they walked the couple of paces to the door. She scrambled to mold her features into an expression that didn't reveal her fear of the unknown future.

Put your trust in the Lord. Those words slipped into her mind. She was trying, but for so long she'd only relied on herself.

"Good night," she murmured after entering the house and crossing to the staircase. "Tell Tyler thanks for watching Jayden and Sara tonight. It was nice getting out by ourselves."

Caleb gave her a quick kiss then stepped back. "He owes me."

On her trek up the stairs she hugged her arms to her, savoring the memory of being in his embrace, experiencing again the feel of his lips on hers.

"I can't believe I got talked into playing Santa Claus. I think the mayor got sick on purpose just so I had to do this." In the church classroom, Caleb turned from the mirror after examining the white beard Annie had glued on his face. "How do I look? Do you think anyone will know it's me?"

Taking in his youthful appearance that the beard couldn't disguise and his dark hair still not completely hidden by the wig, Annie pressed her lips together, trying to contain her laughter. "Yes, but the kids won't. All they'll see is the bundle of presents you're carrying and your jolly belly." Patting his padded stomach in the red suit, she finally released the chuckles she'd held inside since he'd asked her to help him with his beard.

"I'm consoling myself with the fact that this is for a good cause. This party is for the disadvantaged children in the area. The presents I'm delivering will often be all they'll get. This is what makes Christmas so special, giving to others, especially those who don't have anything."

Annie stepped close and adjusted his wig to cover his hair. "Yes, you keep telling yourself that and everything will be fine. You know, I think I have just the right touch to make you look official."

His white eyebrows slashed down. "I don't think I like your tone. What?"

"You're way too suspicious." She rummaged in her purse.

"That's a good thing for a police chief."

She retrieved what she'd been looking for and turned back to him. "And I'm glad. I appreciate all you've done for me, especially bringing the FBI in on what's been going on. With them looking for Salvador for questioning, I feel better."

"Their resources extend further than mine."

"And maybe they'll be able to crack Downey."

"I'm not too sure about that. The man is scared. He's trying not to act that way, but I see it in his expression. According to the FBI, people who cross Salvador die."

"And Bryan somehow had. If Downey worked for Salvador, I can't see Downey killing Salvador's son without him telling him to. Maybe the FBI will find what someone was searching for in my apartment. Bryan could have hidden something there that I'm not aware of."

Caleb gestured toward her balled hand. "What are you hiding there?"

She produced a tube of red lipstick. "This."

His eyes widened. "You want me to wear lipstick?"

She laughed. "Just on the cheeks."

He swiped his hand across his brow. "For a minute I thought you'd gone loco." He fastened on her a pinpoint gaze. "Are you crazy? I'm not wearing lipstick anywhere."

"It might make you look older, disguise you some."

"Well, guess what? Santa has just gotten younger and looks remarkably like Christmas's police chief." With a final glance at the mirror in the church classroom, he headed for the door, grabbing his big, black bag full of presents for the underprivileged. "Let's get this over with, then on to the fireworks celebration. Remember, stay near me."

"Aye, aye, captain." She saluted him.

When Caleb entered the rec room, saying, "Ho ho ho," the kids' eyes brightened, and they rushed toward him, an onslaught of twenty-five children ranging in age from three to ten.

Annie crossed to the kitchen entrance and stood with Sara, watching the joy on the little girls' and boys' faces. Annie spied Jayden with some of the kids from the church standing behind the refreshment tables waiting to serve the food after the gifts were given out. "This is all Jayden talked about today. The party. The presents. She helped make cards to go with the gifts."

"I loved helping y'all bake the sugar cookies today then decorate them. I hadn't done that in years." Sara flashed her a smile. "Look at the turnout. The town does love a good party. I hope we have enough food for everyone."

Annie scanned the large room, full to capacity. Quite a few people she recognized. She wanted to stay in Christmas after the holidays and had prayed about it last night after saying good-night to Caleb. In the short time here, Jayden had blossomed. She trusted Caleb. He believed in her and she'd never really had that.

"Is all the food out?" Annie asked over the claps and giggles coming from the children as Caleb handed out the presents.

"I think so..." Sara snapped her fingers. "Except the dip I stuck in the refrigerator in back. No room in the front one. I forgot about it."

"I'll get it." Annie turned into the entrance. The large kitchen was now empty, but twenty minutes before she'd had a hard time moving around as different church workers took out all the food and made the punch for the party. Making her way around the corner and toward the backup refrigerator and freezer, she listened to the noise coming from the rec hall. Joy. Laughter. The sounds gave her a peace about her decision to stay if the FBI could find Salvador. If not...

She wouldn't think about that right now. Opening the refrigerator door, she saw the large bowl of dip that Sara had prepared for the feast. As she reached for it, a hand snaked around her mouth while an arm slammed her back against a hard body.

"Don't make a sound. I don't have a beef

with anybody else, but if I have to, I'll use my gun. Understand?"

She nodded.

His tanned hand eased from her mouth, but he kept his arm locked about her. Something poked her in the temple, cold and metallic. She slanted her look and nearly collapsed at the sight of the gun to her head.

"We're going for a ride, so we can have a chat undisturbed."

His gravelly voice chilled her to the marrow of her bones.

"If you try anything, I'll shoot you and anyone who tries to interfere. I have nothing to lose."

He dragged her toward the back door at the end of the short hall. That door had been locked earlier but now it stood open. She shouldn't be surprised a criminal knew how to get into a locked building, but surrounded by lots of people she knew and Caleb a room away, she'd felt safe. All an illusion.

At the end of the deserted alley behind the church, a car sat parked. If she got into the vehicle, she would be found dead. She couldn't let that happen.

Chapter Eight

Mobbed by children, Caleb looked toward where Sara and Annie had been talking. Sara stood alone. His gut tightened. Where was Annie? She wasn't supposed to leave his sight. He'd made that clear, and she'd been good about it all day. Either him or a police officer at all times.

"This is my last one." Caleb dug into the bag, grabbing the lone present and pulling it out. "This one is for Danny."

The five-year-old jumped up, waving his arms, with the biggest grin on his face. "I'm Danny."

Caleb waded through the crowd of kids and handed the child his gift, then said, "You can open your presents now."

While they tore into the wrapping, bits of

paper flying everywhere, Caleb covered the distance to Sara. "Where's Annie?"

"She just went into the kitchen to get the dip from the back refrigerator." Sara's forehead scrunched. "She's only been gone a minute or two."

Too long. His gut knotted.

He pivoted into the kitchen and scanned the area. No Annie. He headed toward the back refrigerator. He hurried down the short hallway and checked the refrigerator. The bowl of dip was inside. Slamming the door closed, he went to the exit nearby and tested the handle. Locked.

Caleb swung around, surveying the corridor, and spied the storage room off it. He strode toward the slightly open door.

"What do you want?" Annie asked as Nick Salvador dragged her toward the car. She'd recognized him from a photo in the newspaper.

"I want the information Bryan Daniels had."

"What information?"

The large man stopped a few feet from the vehicle and jerked Annie around to face him. "Don't play dumb with me. He said it was in safekeeping, that if something happened to him it would go to the police. It was photos, a tape and a gun." The laugh that erupted from Salvador's mouth scared her worse than the gun he held in his hand. "Just like in the movies. Fool. He thought I would cower at his threat. I've killed men for less than that."

"I can't give you something I don't have. Your man searched my apartment and didn't find anything."

"It was too important to leave behind. You two probably thought that I would bow down to the blackmail and give him everything he wanted when I didn't accept him as my son."

"But he was your son. How could you send someone after him?"

His laugh froze her. "I can't have children. Never have been able to. He isn't my son. His mother just tried to claim he was."

Bryan, what in the world did you do? Frantic to find a way to convince the man she was telling the truth, she lifted her chin a notch and met his gaze. "Bryan didn't give me anything."

"I know all about your relationship with him. He had no friends. He called you when he knew he would die to tell you to send the information to the police. Downey managed to stop him before he could. I want the information."

What gun, photos and tape? Again she

searched her mind trying to think where or when Bryan would have done that. But all her thoughts centered on the gun Salvador pointed at her.

"Get in." He waved the weapon at the back of the car, then took his key out and popped the trunk.

"In there?" Her squeaky words reverberated through the silence.

"Now." He pushed the lid up and gestured with the gun where he wanted her.

Annie stared at the dark hole he wanted her to crawl into, and fear mushroomed. A band stretched around her chest and contracted. He moved toward her. She scrambled into the trunk before he could lay a hand on her.

The last thing she saw before he slammed the lid was the light at the end of the alley by the closed kitchen door of the church. Then nothing but darkness. Her black surroundings hammered terror into the fiber of her being. Her quaking started in her hands and spread so quickly it consumed her in a matter of seconds.

Sucking in deep breaths that never filled her lungs, she closed her eyes, hoping to trick her mind into thinking she was just resting. But the tight confines pressed in on all sides. Like being in a coffin.

Lord, help. What do I do?

Part of the twenty-third Psalm came to her, weaving its way through her thoughts. *Yea, though I walk through the valley of the shadow of death, I will fear no evil; For You are with me; Your rod and Your staff, they comfort me.* In the wake of those words, calmness cocooned her in a sense of peace. Her rapid breathing slowed.

The motion of the car stopped. Hearing the door shut, Annie braced herself. The trunk popped open and the lid flew up.

"Get out." Salvador stood like an avenger, bent on having his way no matter what it took.

When Annie climbed from the black hole, she hadn't fallen apart as she would have in the past when greeted with darkness like that. Because God was with her. She wasn't alone. Even at the moment when she faced Sara's house, the sense of the Lord's arm about her shoulders cloaked her in a composure she would need if she were going to make it out alive.

"What are we doing here?"

"Your stuff is here. Downey didn't get a chance to go through it. We are now. Either you will give me what I want or I'll kill you. It's that simple."

Caleb, where are you? By now you have to know I'm gone.

"And your cop won't be able to save you. I've got a surprise for him."

The storage area off the kitchen was empty, other than two cigarette butts on the floor by the door. Caleb closed the door and turned into the kitchen. Since he was protecting Annie, he had his service weapon on him. He pulled it out of his holster under his red coat then his cell from his pocket. Had someone been waiting in there? Salvador or someone else he sent?

He called the station. "Tyler, I need you here at the church to watch Jayden and Sara. Annie's gone. I'm going to check the rest of this place. Have Jeremy swing by Sara's house and make sure everything's okay there."

The sound of an explosion roared through his connection. Caleb jerked his cell from his ear for a few seconds before shouting into it, "Tyler, what happened?" Nothing. "Tyler?"

Salvador shoved Annie through the entrance into Sara's house. Suddenly a blast rolled through the air like thunder. She peered behind her and saw a flash light the night toward downtown.

She stopped and pivoted. "What have you done?"

"Got rid of a liability before he decided to talk."

"You blew up the jail?"

He chuckled. "A most effective way to cause a diversion and take out Downey. He had his chance to fix his mistake. He wasn't supposed to kill Bryan until after he got all the information I needed."

I'm a liability, too. Even if I could find the information and give it to him, he'll kill me.

She had to stall as long as she could until someone finally came or she could think of a way out of this situation.

"How did Downey find me?"

Salvador stepped through the entrance and kicked the door closed. "That was easy. Your cop friend led him to you."

Caleb betrayed her? No, he's lying. "You're lying."

The man's laughter erupted. "For once I'm not. He called the Crystal Creek police and introduced himself and then asked about you. If that wasn't enough, he sent someone to check up on you. That someone talked to the police in Crystal Creek about you. It was only a matter of putting a few things together to find where you went. At least Downey was good for something. His police connections helped. Now enough of this, where's your things?"

Again Annie found herself trudging up the stairs to her bedroom with a madman behind her, wanting something she couldn't give him. She and Caleb had discussed what she'd brought and couldn't come up with anything.

At the top of the steps she swung around, and the action was so sudden, it took the man by surprise. His hand shot out and grasped the banister. "Back off." He lifted the gun and pointed it right at her face.

"I don't have what you want. At least tell me why you want them." If she were going to die, she wanted to know why.

He scowled, his eyes narrow. "Bryan's mother, years ago gathered a tape, a gun and photos that tied me to a murder. When she ran away from me, she used it as her insurance to keep me in line. Believe me, I still looked for her, but it's much easier to track a person today than it was twenty-eight years ago."

"Maybe she was lying and there wasn't anything." Bryan certainly had lied to her enough.

"It's possible, but I don't think so. In the note she left me it was clear she knew too much. I don't let people live who know too much about my…affairs." A smile pulled the corners of his mouth in an evil line. "You don't think I know what you're doing. You're stalling. No one's gonna come. Show me your room."

In his vehicle, Caleb called Jeremy. "I need you at the station. The back of the jail was blown up and the fire department is there."

"How's Tyler? He was there."

"Okay. A few cuts and bruises, but he says he can handle the situation. I want you to help him. Downey is dead. Thankfully we didn't have anyone else in jail. Two FBI agents were on the way out of town. They're coming back. They'll help you. I'll take care of Annie."

"Sure, Chief."

Caleb turned down Bethlehem Street and saw Sara's house at the end of the long block. And he also glimpsed an unknown car in front. He gunned his and came to a stop a few seconds later. After confirming Annie wasn't in the church, he knew where Salvador would take her. Annie wouldn't leave the party without letting him know unless the man had taken her.

Thrusting open his door, he hit the ground in a run and headed toward the porch. With his weapon in hand, he snuck into the house.

Pausing in the foyer, he listened, trying to get a feel for where Annie and Salvador were. A floorboard squeaked above the dining room. Annie's bedroom.

He took the stairs two at a time, making sure he avoided a creaky step.

Pages of Bryan's mother's Bible lay scattered all over the bed. Annie's heart pounded in a mad tempo at the sight before her. Every item, even clothing and the suitcases, that she and Jayden had brought from Florida was being torn apart before her eyes. Salvador took hold of the antique porcelain doll Bryan had given her daughter for her birthday last month.

"Please, not Jayden's favorite doll." The words tumbled from her mouth before she could stop them. She knew the man wouldn't listen to her pleas. He hadn't when he'd ripped through the Bible.

He glared at her and proceeded to tear it apart—first the head then the limbs and finally the body. Nothing. He tossed it down at his feet. "That's it. Everything." He scanned the room. "How about that?" He pointed at the ceramic Christmas tree nearby.

"Not mine."

He picked it up and smashed it against the

floor then toed the pieces to see if there was anything hidden among them. His scowl deepened into an almost desperate look when he peered toward her. "It's got to be here. I've looked everywhere I could—Bryan's apartment and car, anything I could tie to him. You're my last link." He covered the few feet between them and slammed her up against the wall by the bed. "Where is it? You've hidden it in this house. If I have to and can't find it, I'll burn this place down rather than let anyone find the evidence. I don't leave evidence around to be used against me." His hand gripped her neck as he held her pinned with his body.

Nor witnesses, from all she'd read about him. "Bryan never gave me anything that would hold photos, a tape and a gun. Believe me, I would know that."

"Maybe it's something smaller—a note about the location of where the items are." Frustration toughened his voice to a growl.

Frantic, she searched the chaotic mess strewn about the room and zeroed in on Jayden's treasure chest sitting undisturbed on the dresser, as though part of Sara's belongings. Salvador squeezed her neck, the glint in his eyes feral.

Slowly he cut the flow of air to her lungs. Her mind swirled from the lack of oxygen.

"Box," she choked out, shifting her gaze to the item on the dresser, peeking out from some clothing pitched onto its top.

He eased the pressure about her burning throat. "Where?"

"Dresser." She dragged air into her oxygen-starved lungs as his hand fell away and he turned toward the piece of furniture a few feet away.

Quickly crossing to it, he snatched it up and lifted the lid, throwing Jayden's treasures— a polished rock, a picture of her, Bryan and Jayden, a necklace, her favorite hair ribbons— onto the floor. He checked the box's bottom, but it was solid wood, then his gaze latched on to the satin lining of the lid. He ripped it off and a key and a piece of paper fell out.

As he picked them up, flinging the box to the side, Annie saw her chance while his attention was riveted on the small paper. She grabbed the alarm clock on the nightstand next to her and swung toward Salvador. He started to turn toward her when she smashed the metal-and-plastic object into his head as hard as she could. He swayed.

Then she ran as quickly as she could for the

door. His curses propelled her faster and faster as she hit the hallway and saw the staircase only ten feet away.

Caleb heard the sound of pounding foot-steps coming toward him as he climbed the stairs. He swung toward the noise, and through the slats in the banister he saw Annie. He increased his speed. She rushed toward him, her eyes wide, her face pale. Then she spied him and lengthened her strides even more.

He looked behind her. Salvador emerged from her bedroom, his expression contorted with rage. The man planted his feet and lifted his Glock, aiming for Annie. Caleb stopped and sighted Salvador through the railing.

Caleb squeezed off his shot a split second before Salvador could. Annie dove the last few feet toward the staircase. Salvador's bullet whizzed by her and hit the wall. Caleb's struck the man in the chest. Salvador staggered back, tried to lift his arm to shoot again, but Caleb fired again and Salvador crumbled to the floor.

Caleb scrambled up the two remaining steps and gathered Annie into his arms. "Are you okay?"

Tears streaked down her face. She threw her arms around his neck and sobbed.

* * *

"May I have a word with you, Annie?" Caleb's voice held no emotion in it.

She paused and turned from the front door as Sara and Jayden were finally allowed into the house after the scene upstairs had been processed and Salvador's body carted off. "Sure. Jayden, can you go with Miss Sara for a few minutes? I won't be long."

"I've got some cookies left over from church tonight and some milk. Wanna share some with me?" Sara offered her hand to Jayden. "Then I imagine you'll want to take a hot bath. You and your mom are gonna camp out downstairs in the living room. Won't that be fun!"

Jayden hesitated, clinging to Annie.

"I won't keep her but a few minutes. I just need to check out some things." Although Caleb grinned at Jayden, a tic twitched right above his jaw line.

"Mommy, I'll save a coupla cookies for you."

"And some milk." Jayden didn't know what had happened that evening upstairs. Sara had kept her at the church helping to clean up. Annie would have to explain part of it to her daughter. The past hours had been filled with people in and out, and all she wanted to do was collapse on the portable mattress Caleb had set up for her and Jayden and sleep for the next twenty-four hours.

Jayden leaned back and looked up at Annie. "Okay?"

"I am, honey. I just had some things I had to take care of here at the house, but everything's okay now. Enjoy the snack."

Jayden fit her hand in Sara's while the older lady kept a running commentary going about how successful the Christmas party at the church was and what a big help Jayden had been.

"Let's go into the living room," Caleb said in that matter-of-fact voice he'd been using since that brief time he'd held her at the top of the stairs and let her cry.

When she settled on the couch, he remained standing, facing her. "Why did you leave the rec hall this evening? What part of 'you need to stay with me at all times' did you not understand? He had you in his sights tonight. You could be dead right now instead of Salvador. You could—" Frustration and anger poured off Caleb, his hands curling into fists and uncurling at his sides.

He was angry with her for going into the kitchen when he was the reason it all happened. She drew herself up tall, lifting her chin a notch. "I know exactly how Downey found me. Salvador told me you sent someone to Crystal Creek to check up on me. What did you think? I was a criminal running from the law?" When guilt flickered across his face, his gaze sliding away for a few seconds, her own fury surfaced. "You did think that."

"No, not really, but I could tell you were in trouble, and you weren't talking."

"It wasn't any of your business."

"Ah, the 'I can do everything by myself' attitude. How far did it get you today?"

His question wounded her more than she ever wanted him to know. She narrowed her eyes and pinned him with her look. "I've learned the hard way not to depend on others."

"And yet today, you had to."

She fisted her hands. "Yes, today I did. But that's not the issue here. You didn't trust me, or you wouldn't have gone digging into my life." Annie surged to her feet, needing to get away from the anger she saw in his eyes. "I have a daughter who needs me. Good night." She strode toward the foyer and opened the front door for him.

He walked passed her without looking at her. He stopped, started to turn back. Quickly she shut the door, too tired to go into her feelings concerning Caleb. She half expected him to pound on the wood and demand she let him in. But he didn't, which spoke volumes to her.

How did she expect him to be any different from Bryan? He had her investigated, so when she was spilling her guts to him, he'd known all about her past.

"Is Jayden finally asleep?" Sara asked in the kitchen, where she was cleaning up after their snack.

"Yes, I laid down with her and held her until she drifted off." Annie collapsed into a chair at the table, too weary even to sleep with her daughter in the living room on the air mattress. When she'd tried to close her eyes, all she saw was Caleb's furious face.

"Did you tell her anything about what happened tonight?"

"Not yet, but I'll have to tomorrow when she sees all her things were destroyed. I just couldn't deal with it after…" After the scene with Caleb.

"How about you?" Sara sat across from Annie.

"I've made a mess of everything. Caleb is mad at me for leaving the rec hall." Tears blurred her vision.

"That's his frustration lashing out. He was frantic when he couldn't find you this evening. He kept saying he shouldn't have been Santa. I think he blames himself for everything that happened."

"It wasn't his fault. It wasn't mine, either. Salvador would have come after me one way or another. He was crazed. I'm glad the FBI took the safety deposit key and the box's location. Let them deal with what's in it. Not that it makes much difference, since Salvador is dead. So much death." She shuddered, several tears rolling down her cheeks. She didn't even try to stop them. "I can't believe Bryan hid something so potentially dangerous in one of Jayden's possessions."

"What are you gonna do now? You have a home here for as long as you want."

"I don't know. I guess I could go back to Crystal Creek, but that never really felt like my home. What do I do about Caleb? I care for him so much."

"It's sounding like much more than that. Are you falling in love with him?"

"I—yes."

"You won't find a better man."

"I know, but we can't have a relationship without total trust. And I don't think he really trusts me. He had me investigated like a criminal."

Sara peered down at the table then up into Annie's eyes. "I think I had a part in that happening. I told him I thought you were in trouble. He said he would do some poking around and see what he could find out. I'm so sorry. It wasn't that I didn't trust you. I was worried about you. You weren't sleeping. I could tell something was really troubling you. Please forgive me."

"Always. You have been so kind to me and Jayden." Annie reached across the table and covered Sara's hand. "I'm still not sure how much Caleb really can put his trust in someone. For that matter me. I've been so scared to do that, especially after Bryan. After years of not trusting others, I finally trusted Bryan and let him get close. Look what happened because of that. He put me in danger as well as his daughter." She averted her gaze, the scene with Salvador replaying in her mind.

"Do you trust the Lord?"

Do I? The whole time she'd been with Salvador she'd prayed to God to protect her. And He had. He'd answered her prayers and had even given her a sense of peace in the midst of her panic in the trunk. She used to think He'd forsaken her because of her past, but He hadn't. He'd been with her the whole time, even at the end, when she'd dove toward the staircase. Something instinctively had compelled her to drop suddenly. "Yes, I do. I couldn't have said that a few weeks ago."

"Then trust He's there for you always. Turn your dilemma over to Him concerning Caleb. Ask Him for His advice on what to do."

Annie pushed to her feet and came to Sara, giving the older woman a hug. "I will. Thanks for listening. Thanks for opening your home to Jayden and me."

"You've helped this old lady feel young again. I should be thanking you."

Annie trudged into the living room, wishing she could collapse onto the makeshift bed but knowing from past experience she wouldn't. One light still on, she found Sara's Bible on the end table by Sara's lounge chair and let it fall open. Annie began reading the first chapter of Nahum.

The Lord is good, a strong hold in the day of trouble; and He knoweth them that trust in Him.

As in the trunk, a peace descended as she continued to read the Lord's words. Had He led her to Christmas? To Sara and Caleb? She'd come to care for the people in this town in a short amount of time.

The next evening when Annie saw Caleb come home from work, she hurried down to his house and rang his bell. When he opened his door, she drank in the sight of the man she loved and was determined to fight for. Shadows under his eyes declared the toll the past few weeks had taken on Caleb. The urge to throw her arms around him inundated her, but the closed expression on his face stopped her.

"May I come in?"

He stepped to the side. "Have you come to tell me you're going back to Crystal Creek now that you're free of Salvador?"

"What if I told you I wanted to stay in Christmas?" Her heartbeat accelerated as she tried to read his emotions behind his neutral countenance. "Would you mind?"

"You don't need my permission." Wariness still touched his voice, but there was a warmth inching into it.

"I know, but I felt like we should talk about it."

"For how long?"

"Talking or staying?"

"Staying."

Hearing the note of hurt in his words and remembering about his past relationship with the woman in Tulsa, she advanced toward him. "I'm staying for good. I don't want to move on or go back to Crystal Creek. I want to call Christmas my home. But I don't want to stay if it'll make you uncomfortable or—"

He reached and dragged her the remaining few feet to him. "You mean that? You want to live in Christmas?"

"Yes. I love the town, the people—but especially you." She peered up into his endearing face, seeing his neutral expression melt into a look of joy.

"Say that again."

"I love you, Caleb. I know last night we were both exhausted, upset at how close we came to the outcome being different. I want us to trust totally in each other. That takes time. I want to stay and fight for your love."

He framed her face, burying his fingers in her hair. "You don't have to fight for my love. You have it already." He brushed his lips across hers. "You really didn't do anything wrong last night at church. I think toward the end when everyone was leaving the crime scene I began to figure you had nothing to hold you in Christmas, that you'd want to go back to Florida and pick up your old life. I began to distance myself from you because I didn't want to be hurt again. I started to come by several times today, but I just couldn't bring myself to find you packing or for you to tell me you were leaving, so I stayed away."

"I trust you with my heart. I'm not going anywhere." She pulled his mouth down onto hers and kissed him.

Epilogue

Jayden rushed into Annie and Caleb's bedroom. "C'mon, Mom. It's almost time for the celebration to start. We can't be late. You're supposed to turn the lights on the Christmas tree tonight."

When the town council had given her the honor of being the Mistress of the Festival of Lights, she'd been surprised and speechless. Her husband of ten months had accepted before she could get the words out of her mouth. "I'm coming. Where's Caleb?"

"He went ahead and picked up Miss Sara since you were taking forever."

Her daughter disappeared, but her pounding footsteps could be heard throughout the house as she went down the stairs. She had grown up so much in the year they had lived in Christmas. Annie pushed herself to her feet, her back hurting. She placed her hand on her rounded stomach and felt the baby kick beneath it. He was going to play soccer or maybe football. Caleb would like that. He'd already bought some sports equipment, but it would be years until their son would be big enough to use any of it.

"It won't be too much longer. Maybe you'll be a New Year's baby. I know your daddy can't wait."

As fast as she could she made her way to the front door, grabbed her overcoat and shrugged into it. A minute later she sat in the passenger seat of an SUV that Caleb had recently purchased for his expanding family.

Annie peered in the back and gave Sara a smile. "It's gonna snow tonight. I feel it in the air."

"Perfect. A little snow during our opening celebration would add just the right touch." Sara patted Jayden's hand on the seat between them. "Don't you think?"

"Yeah. I love making snowmen."

"If so, I'll probably have to work later helping people." Caleb threw Annie a warm look.

Sara chuckled. "The townspeople aren't too great driving on snow. Maybe it'll hold off until everyone's home for the night."

When Caleb parked near the town square,

where the huge Christmas tree was erected, Jayden thrust open the door, saying, "I see Lisa. Be back in a minute."

"I don't think I'll see her for the rest of the evening," Annie muttered, watching her child disappearing into the middle of a group of children.

Sara pushed open her door and slowly stood, reaching in for her plate of goodies. "I'll be at the refreshment table if y'all need me."

"Mrs. Jackson, we're finally alone." Caleb took her hand and lifted it to his lips to kiss her knuckles.

"But not for long. Isn't that the mayor heading for us?"

Caleb scanned the crowd amassing around the square. "I do believe it is." He tugged Annie toward him. "Let's give him something to talk about."

Her husband settled his mouth over hers and kissed her long and hard while the revelry took place around them. When he leaned back slightly, a smile encompassed his whole face.

He smoothed her hair back behind her ears. "I'm thinking the Mistress of the Festival of Lights is now properly charged and ready to do her duty."

* * * * *

Dear Reader,

It was interesting mixing Christmas and suspense in this story. It wasn't as easy as I thought at the beginning. When I think of Christmas, I don't think of dead bodies, villains and crime. Although it was an unexpected challenge, I was glad I was asked to write this novella to go in a book with one by Debby Giusti. I was honored to be paired with Debby. She is a wonderful romantic suspense writer.

I love hearing from readers. You can contact me at margaretdaley@gmail.com or at P.O. Box 2074 Tulsa, OK 74101. You can also learn more about my books at www.margaret-daley.com. I have a quarterly newsletter that you can sign up for on my website or you can enter my monthly drawings by signing my guestbook.

Best wishes,

Margaret Daley

Questions for Discussion

1. Annie thought God had forsaken her because of the mistakes she'd made in the past. Have you felt this way? Why? What happened?

2. What is your favorite scene? Why?

3. Trust is an issue for both Annie and Caleb. How important is trust in a relationship to you? Why do you feel that way?

4. Annie is naive about ways to protect herself against a man like Nick Salvador. Do you feel confident about protecting yourself? Why or why not?

5. Who is your favorite character? Why?

6. What lengths would you go to in order to protect your child? A loved one?

7. Caleb takes care of Sara as a good friend. What are some things we can do to help the elderly in our society?

8. By investigating Annie, Caleb put her in danger without meaning to. Have you ever

done something that put someone in danger or in a situation that was unpleasant for that person? What happened?

YULE DIE

Debby Giusti

To my mother,
Betty Willoughby,
With love and gratitude

Behold, the virgin shall be with child
and bear a son, and they shall name him Emmanuel,
which means God is with us.
–*Matthew* 1:23

Chapter One

"Christmas should be a time of joy, not sorrow," Callie Evans whispered as she pulled into the parking spot directly behind Lazarus House. The news she'd just heard over the radio made her heart heavy. Reaching for the control knob, she paused to listen to the rest of the report.

"Two of the three gunmen wounded in yesterday's east Atlanta shootout died during the night," the announcer said. "Hospital personnel decline to comment on the lone survivor."

Callie sighed with regret. Turning off the radio, she climbed from the Magnolia Medical van, dropped the keys into the pocket of her lab coat and hustled up the rear steps of the nursing home. Without warning, her mind flashed back fifteen years to another Christmas—the unlatched gate, the swollen pond, her sister's tiny body.

Stamping her feet to ward off the bitter cold and the memory, Callie opened the back door, stepped inside and hurried toward the narrow front lobby.

Nurse Tamika Bryant's broad face cracked into a welcoming grin and her eyes twinkled like the lights on the small tree in the corner. "You're amazing to help us out on Christmas Eve."

Callie smiled back at the day-shift supervisor. Tamika had a heart big enough to embrace the fifteen men who, without family to love them, found comfort and care under her watchful eye.

"Mr. Petrecelli needs a digoxin level drawn, and we've got a new guy in room seven." Tamika handed her the lab request forms.

Opening the storage cabinet, Callie grabbed the bulky phlebotomy tray and glanced at the slips. "Harry Potter? It's a joke, right?"

Tamika's smile faded. "Atlanta Police Department's idea of humor. They're trying to keep the guy's identity under wraps. He was involved in that shootout on Foster Street yesterday."

Callie had heard the initial report on the television last night. "The news mentioned a lone survivor."

The nurse nodded. "That's our guy. He had surgery at Grady Hospital. According to the night-shift supervisor, they transported him here at two this morning when the cops got word his pals wanted to spring him. Rumor has it the Exterminators were involved."

"But why would the police bring him here?"

"To hide him from his Exterminator buddies." Tamika pursed her lips. "Look, if you don't feel comfortable, I can draw his blood."

Callie shook her head. "No. It's okay."

"Offer up one of those prayers you're famous for. Maybe you can change his heart."

Callie smiled then glanced around, seeing none of the aides who usually worked the weekend shift. "Where is everyone?"

"Sam called in sick, and Barb got tied up in that holiday parade snaking though the city."

"Santa and his elves. A little ho-ho-ho on Christmas Eve."

Tamika lifted her brow. "That invitation still holds. You know we'd love to have you spend Christmas with us."

"Thanks, but my brother called a few days ago and asked if he could come over."

The nurse's eyes widened. "You haven't seen Robbie in years."

"Three to be exact. I'm not sure what he wants. He didn't have time to chat."

Tamika smiled. "Maybe his sister's good influence finally rubbed off on him."

"Either that or he needs money and thinks he can rip me off again."

"I hear you. Someone who took my credit card and treated himself to a weekend fling wouldn't find me welcoming him back with open arms."

But Callie's arms weren't open. They were crossed over her chest and her foot was tapping with a "let's see if you've changed" attitude.

Truth was, despite what he'd done, Callie loved her younger brother. Separated as kids when their parents divorced, Callie had drawn the short end of the straw. Not that her mother had been a bad woman, just unforgiving.

Her mother had cut all ties with the male side of the family, changing her last name and Callie's to spite the husband who'd wronged her. Then, true to her narcissistic nature, she'd heaped the underlying blame on her daughter's shoulders. Callie accepted the guilt for her sister's death but not for her parents' failed marriage.

"I told Robbie to come back when he straightened out his life." Callie arranged the Vacutainer tubes on her tray. "Maybe he has."

The head nurse shrugged. "Things don't work out tomorrow, you come over to my house. You know James and the girls consider you family."

"I've got presents for the kids. I'll drop them off after church in the morning."

"You're spoiling them for sure." The phone rang and Tamika reached for the receiver as Callie placed the lab slips on her tray and headed down the side corridor.

She'd draw the new guy's blood first then spend time with Mr. Petrecelli, a cancer patient who could use a visitor, especially on Christmas Eve. Tamika had mentioned an anonymous donor who, unbeknownst to Theo, took care of his medical expenses. The only other person in his life was an estranged brother. She and Theo would pray for his younger sibling as they always did. *Please, Lord, bring him back into Theo's life.*

Glancing out the window, Callie noted the string of older homes lining the neighboring residential streets. Someone in the Atlanta PD must have realized the out-of-the-way care facility would be the last place the gang would look for their buddy.

Rounding the corner, Callie saw the officer sitting on a folding chair at the end of the hallway. Face flushed, the guy packed at least twenty pounds of extra weight along with his weapon. Hopefully, he had Christmas off to spend with his family.

The cop stood as she neared. "I've gotta check your tray, ma'am."

"Don't bother." Callie pointed to a bookcase in the nearby alcove. "I'll grab what I need and leave everything else out here." She shoved a needle and three Vacutainer collection tubes into the pocket of her lab coat along with a tourniquet, alcohol swab and a bandage. After placing the metal tray on the bookshelf, she stepped through the door the cop held open for her.

Closed venetian blinds covered the window, throwing the room into shadow. The patient lay under a pile of blankets, face to the wall, his chest rising and falling in sync with the labored pull of air through his lungs.

"Sir?" Nearing the bed, she touched his arm. "I need to draw your blood."

The patient groaned then shifted and turned toward her.

Callie's heart hydroplaned against her chest. "Robbie?"

Chapter Two

Joe Petrecelli drew in a lungful of cold December air and checked his watch. He'd run the two miles from his condo in fourteen minutes. Not his personal best, but decent and a strong indication he'd max the annual PT test again this year. Unless some dirtbag perpetrator decided to do a little target practice with Joe in his sights.

Seven years on the force, and he'd been lucky. A flesh wound to the shoulder and a broken collarbone. Not bad, when he considered the odds.

Joe had the holiday weekend off, but he'd be back at his desk by 9:00 a.m. after he jogged home to shower and change out of his sweats. Not that anyone expected him at work.

He glanced up and down the street. Quiet.

No traffic. He'd been right. Lazarus House was a safe hideaway. God willing, the Exterminators wouldn't find their man here. Not that the Lord had much control over the gang of extortionists ravaging Joe's part of the metro area. Still, he wouldn't turn down help no matter where it originated, even from a God he'd shoved aside years ago.

Pulling open the front door and stepping into the warm interior, Joe made a mental note to call headquarters for more security. The nursing home was out of the way, but he wouldn't underestimate the Exterminators.

One nurse on duty. Joe flashed his badge, and the woman pointed him toward the side corridor, not realizing he'd been there in the middle of the night when the patient transported over from Grady.

Joe's footsteps sounded on the polished hardwood. He spied Phil Rogers, pulling duty at the end of the hallway. Glancing beyond the cop to room 10, Joe's gut tightened. Theo's room.

He still couldn't forgive his older brother. Joe had been thirteen when their parents died. He'd expected Theo—twenty-one and living on his own—to be his guardian. Instead, Theo had moved on with his life of carousing and drunkenness and abandoned Joe when he'd needed his brother the most. Forced into foster care, Joe had vowed to cut all ties with his self-centered sibling, and to this day, the two brothers had never met face-to-face again.

Acknowledging the officer on duty, Joe stepped into the patient's room and closed the door behind him. Movement caught his eye. He turned.

A woman stood in the shadows. White lab coat, swarm of black curls, alabaster skin. Troubled blue eyes captured his gaze.

Joe's gut tightened and warmth flooded over him. He spied the tourniquet in her clenched fist and tried to override the conflicting signals pinging against his heart.

Glancing at the patient, he asked, "Is the kid okay?"

"He...he appears stable." She stepped into the light.

Pretty, in a fresh, wholesome way, the woman stared back at him with an intensity that made his world shift.

Instantly aware of his own less-than-stellar appearance, he glanced down at his sweats, wishing he'd already showered and shaved. Needing to introduce himself, Joe pulled out the leather case he carried on his waistband in lieu of a wallet and held out his badge and police identification.

"Atlanta PD," he said, as if that would explain the reason he'd ventured into the patient's room.

She took the case.

A name tag hung from her lab coat. Callie Evans, MT(ASCP). Magnolia Medical.

Atlanta's state-of-the-art laboratory complex. Joe hadn't expected their techs to work at the home.

"Joseph X. Petrecelli." She read his name off the ID then glanced up as if seeing him clearly for the first time. Her eyes appeared almost turquoise.

"Joseph *Xavier* Petrecelli?" Her forehead wrinkled. "You're Theo's baby brother?"

Now Joe was the one to furrow his brow.

"Room ten," she continued. "Three doors down on the left."

Before Joe could respond, a scuffle sounded in the hallway. Joe hesitated for a second too long. The door crashed open.

Callie's eyes widened and the badge fell from her fingers and slipped under the bed.

Joe stepped in front of her. His hand searched for the service revolver he'd left back at his condo. Stupid mistake. Dropping to the floor, he pulled Callie down with him and reached for the .38 strapped to his calf.

Not fast enough.

Three men stormed into the room armed with automatics. Black ski masks covered their faces. Latex gloves encased their hands.

The tallest of the three kicked Joe beneath the eye.

"Augh!" Thrown off balance, the gun flew from his grasp. Joe grabbed the bedrail, pulled himself upright and lunged, crashing into the torso of the lanky guy who belonged to the boot. He followed with a fist to the guy's gut.

Callie screamed. The shortest of the three men wrapped his arm across her chest and jammed an automatic to her head.

"Let her go." Joe went for the gun.

A stocky guy slammed the butt of his pistol into Joe's neck.

Callie's mouth opened, but the ringing in his ears muffled her screams. Joe gasped for air.

The tall guy twisted Joe's arms behind his back, forcing him upright and opening his airway.

The patient's eyes blinked open. He struggled to rise off the bed.

"No," Joe warned, earning a knee to the

small of his back. He doubled over, his face close to the kid's ear. "Don't move!"

Hands jerked Joe away.

The stocky perpetrator appeared in charge. He pointed his gun at Callie. "Rocky needs medical care. You come with us."

"What about the jock?" the short gunman asked. Deep voice, Latino accent.

The leader turned his eyes—piercing slits in the otherwise faceless mask—on Joe.

"Kill him."

Chapter Three

"You'll need help moving the patient." Joe grasped for anything that could slow down the action. "Leave the woman. Take me instead."

"He smells like a cop, Arnie," the Latino snarled. "He was packing a snub nose in his ankle holster."

Arnie? Arnie Frazier? One of the Exterminators' chief musclemen. *Keep talking,* Joe thought. *Draw attention off the woman.*

"Must be the sweat you're smelling." Joe's lips twisted into a grin. "The gun's for protection. Did you get a look at the neighborhood around here?"

Callie's face blanched. Her eyes glazed with fear. His first priority was to get her out of the mix.

"The woman's bound to slow you down," Joe continued. "Lock her in the latrine."

"Sanchez, I told you to kill him," Arnie spat back at the Latino.

"But he's a…?" Callie glanced at Joe for help. "A doctor."

Doctor was good. At least she hadn't mentioned he was a cop.

"You need both of us to keep Robbie alive." She struggled to free herself from Sanchez's hold.

"His name's Rocky," the Latino sneered, jerking her back against his chest.

Arnie turned to the tall dude. "Frisk him, Malachi." Joe clenched his jaw while the guy patted him down.

"He's clean."

Where was Rogers, the guard? Bound and gagged? Or dead?

Malachi shoved Joe toward the bed. "You carry Rocky."

"He…he's just had surgery," Callie pleaded. "There's a transport gurney in the alcove."

"She's right," Joe seconded, not that they appeared interested in anything he had to say.

"Please," she begged.

Arnie aimed the gun at Joe. He got the message. Wrapping one arm under the patient's shoulders and the other beneath his knees, Joe raised the kid off the mattress, making the shift as smooth as possible.

Malachi stepped into the hallway. The Latino followed, shoving Callie ahead of him.

Arnie eyed Joe. "You're next."

Holding the wounded patient, Joe moved forward. The guard lay in the alcove. His chest moved but only slightly. He needed medical care stat.

Arnie jammed the gun into Joe's back. "Keep walking."

The entourage snaked along the hallway toward the lobby, where the nurse sat slumped over her desk. Blood stained her scrubs, verifying her need for immediate medical care, as well. She moaned.

Ten steps to the back door. Joe ran through their options.

Get outside where someone would see them. A passing motorist. A next-door neighbor.

Take it slow and easy. Buy time.

Any distraction could be the opportunity they'd need to escape.

"You got a car big enough for all of us?" Joe asked, doubtful the thugs drove a minivan. He hoped his question would throw them off track.

The Latino looked back over his shoulder.

Joe shrugged, a smirk on his lips. "Sorry, guys, but I left my wheels at home."

Malachi inched open the back door. A white utility van with the words *Magnolia Medical* painted on the side panel sat at the base of the steps. The tall gunman glanced at Callie's name tag, making the connection.

"Looks like the woman can help us out," Malachi said.

Joe's optimism deflated. He caught Callie's gaze. *Do what they say, honey,* he tried to warn her. The terror he saw in her eyes made him realize she was scared to death.

The patient struggled in Joe's arms, his breathing labored. Death hovered close to him. Close to all of them.

If Joe didn't do something and do it fast, three of the six people walking out of Lazarus House wouldn't live to see Christmas day.

The cold air whipped around Callie as she stumbled down the back steps, urged on by the gunman's hand around her upper arm. She jerked away from his touch.

"Watch it, lady," he growled.

Squaring her shoulders, she shoved out her jaw with determination. No matter how much she was trembling inside, she wouldn't let them see her fear.

Once again, she glanced over her shoulder at the cop, a man she'd prayed for countless times with Theo. Cancer had wasted the older brother's body into soft flesh that hung on a bony frame. In contrast, Joe was bulk and brawn and raw emotion that made her heart quicken and her pulse race. Dark eyes matched his hair and the shadow of beard that outlined his angled jaw.

Theo sought forgiveness and a chance to reconnect with the brother who couldn't forgive the sins of his past. Something Callie and Joe shared in common. They'd both shut out their siblings and closed the doors to their hearts. Although every time she caught Joe's gaze, her door creaked open.

When Callie had approached her brother's bed earlier to draw his blood, Robbie had shown no sign of recognizing her. Probably the post-surgery medication coupled with the seriousness of his injury.

Now his body hung limp in Joe's arms. Robbie's prognosis couldn't be good. Concern for her brother enveloped her like a winter fog. How had he gotten involved with these despicable men?

And Tamika? Would she survive her injuries?

The guard? *Oh, Lord, help all of them.*

Callie had left her purse and her cell phone in the van. Maybe she could call 9-1-1.

But how? *Think. Think.*

"Keys?" The guy at her side held out his right hand. His left tightened on her arm.

"In my pocket." She slipped her hand into her lab coat, pulled out the bundle of keys and dropped it into his outstretched palm. He unlocked the rear door. Plastic containers filled with supplies cluttered the transport area in the rear of the van.

"Clean out the back so we can lie Rocky down." Sanchez nudged her forward.

Hands trembling, she stacked the plastic interlocking containers and shoved them aside. A thin pad of industrial carpet covered the floor.

"I've got a coat in the front passenger seat," she said. "Toss it back here."

The tall guy did as she asked. Callie arranged her wrap and helped the cop place Robbie on the makeshift pallet. Her shoulder rubbed against Joe's, sending a jolt of awareness through her body. Dwarfed by his size, she was surprised by his control in the midst of chaos. His fingers touched hers and a surge of hope coursed through her veins. At least they were in this together.

"Don't do anything foolish," he whispered, his voice low, determined. "I'll take care of everything."

Callie nodded ever so slightly, noting the flecks of gold that rimmed his eyes. His left cheek looked bruised and swollen. A gash marked his neck, but his smile of encouragement warmed her in spite of the frigid wind that swirled around them.

She pulled a blanket from one of the crates that contained supplies for blood draws and covered her brother. Joe started to climb into the rear to adjust the fabric.

Arnie grabbed his shoulder. "No way, buddy. You drive."

Joe stepped back and supported Callie's elbow as she crawled in next to Robbie. Releasing her arm, his fingers swept against the small of her back before he stepped to the front of the van.

The assurance in his touch strengthened Callie's resolve. If they worked together, they'd get out of this alive. Refocusing her attention on the problem at hand, she tucked the blanket around her brother, keeping her gaze on anything except the handbag wedged in the corner.

Sanchez hoisted himself onto the bench seat. Malachi slipped in beside him. The cop and the other man claimed the captain's chairs up front, the bulky guy riding shotgun. He tugged his ski mask off his face and discarded the latex gloves. He was white, middle-aged, his faced pocked with scars. Probably acne as a kid.

"Pull onto the street, turn left and take it nice and slow," he said to Joe.

The engine turned over and hummed to life. The two men directly ahead of her ripped off their masks and gloves. The tall guy, Malachi, had mahogany skin, short hair and a slender face that fit his lanky body. He glanced back, his black eyes flicking from her to Robbie. He was close to her brother's age. Twenty-three, twenty-four.

Probably ten years older, Sanchez had a round face, square jaw and black hair. His skin appeared a few shades lighter than Malachi's but still dark.

Sanchez turned to check on her, his eyes scanning the rear of the van. "Whatcha doing, lady?"

"Taking care of my—" no reason to let them know Robbie was her brother "—my patient."

"You treat him real good, make sure he stays alive. Okay, doll?"

"I'm not your doll."

He glanced at her name tag. "Easy, Callie. You cool down. Don't give me no trouble. You understand?"

Joe's gaze caught hers in the rearview mirror. At this distance, she couldn't read him. Maybe he was telling her to keep quiet.

Callie wiped her hand over Robbie's cheek. His skin felt warm. Infections often followed surgery. No telling what had entered his body along with the bullet.

Sanchez shifted and glanced nervously out the front window, giving her time to dig into her handbag. Her fingers touched the cool metal of her cell. Hopefully, the gunman wouldn't hear the call go through.

The van bounced along the road. Callie could feel the ruts in the pavement. The jarring motion wouldn't help her brother.

Malachi said something to the Latino.

Now or never.

She tapped in 9-1-1 and pushed Send.

"Emergency Operations Center. Please state your problem." The operator's voice sounded from the phone.

Callie glanced at the men up front. Had they heard anything?

Sanchez turned, perhaps sensing her gaze. "You say something, doll?"

He spied the phone. Spanish expletives flew from his mouth, and he yanked the cell from her hand.

Arnie looked back. "What's goin' on?"

The Latino held up the phone.

"Toss it," the leader ordered.

Sanchez rolled down the window and threw the phone into a wooded area. Swiveling to face her, he raised his hand and struck Callie across the jaw.

She reeled back, and her head slammed against the wall of the van.

"Next time you do something loco," Sanchez sneered, "you'll die."

Chapter Four

Adrenaline shot through Joe. He swerved to the side of the road, stomped on the brake and turned ready to pound some sense into Sanchez. "Don't touch her."

Arnie jammed the muzzle of his gun into Joe's side.

"So, Doc, you wanna be a martyr?"

Joe wanted to shove his fist down Sanchez's throat, but that wouldn't help the situation. Callie needed protection, not a hotheaded madman who would make matters worse.

Clamping down on his jaw, Joe pivoted forward, grabbed the wheel and ground his foot onto the accelerator. Gas surged through the engine. The tires screamed in protest.

Sanchez cursed from the backseat. The fingers of Arnie's left hand snaked around Joe's neck. His right hand forced the gun deeper into Joe's side.

"Blow off steam again—" the warning shot from Arnie's mouth "—and the girl dies."

Joe flicked his gaze to the side mirror. "An SUV's passing on the left. My advice is, you take your hands off my neck."

"He's right," Sanchez said. "A guy and his two kids. Christmas tree strapped to the roof."

Arnie's fingers released their hold. He adjusted himself in the passenger seat, keeping his gun low.

Joe eased up on the accelerator so the SUV could pass. No reason for the man and his kids to suspect anything amiss. They didn't need to get involved. Let them have their merry Christmas. Too many people had already been hurt by the Exterminators.

Once again, Joe looked in the rearview mirror. Callie stared back at him. The mark of Sanchez's hand was on her jaw. Tears glistened in her eyes, but she blinked to keep them in check.

A sense of helplessness swept over Joe. He had to bide his time. Outnumbered, without a weapon, he couldn't let his emotions get the best of him. He had to use every bit of training and experience to outsmart the three gunmen and gain control of the situation. The wounded patient was important, but Joe's number-one priority was to get Callie Evans out of the situation alive.

Callie's jaw burned where Sanchez had slapped her, but what hurt worse was seeing her brother's declining condition and the worry that they might kill Joe. Surely a cop would know to play along with the bad guys until an opportunity arose to escape. She didn't have a degree in criminal justice, but she'd watched enough cop shows on TV. Keep the bad guys thinking they were in control. Try to establish a relationship with them so they'd let their guard down. With a gun aimed at his heart, this wasn't the time to be Mr. Macho Cool.

Of course, Callie hadn't followed her own advice. Making a 9-1-1 cell call had been a risk, and she'd been caught. That was her mistake—at least the being-caught part. She'd seen a story on a television reenactment about a carjacked woman who'd done the same thing. Only that gunman had been oblivious to the call and the woman had been saved.

To save Robbie, she needed Joe's help. Callie looked down at her brother. For all the trouble he was in, Robbie might not want help. He seemed to be in league with these gang members. If they got out of this situation alive, he'd have to face the consequences of his crimes.

He'd been a kid when their parents separated. It was doubtful their dad had been the best of role models. A bitter man, he'd been verbally abusive, often scoffed at the concept of a loving God and died without a change of heart.

No wonder Robbie had made bad choices. Callie hadn't helped. For all her talk about God's love, she'd turned her back on her brother three years ago when their mother had died. Callie should have surrounded him with love. Maybe then, he would have been able to turn his life around.

Callie looked forward, once again catching Joe's gaze in the rearview mirror. The cop seemed to glance back more than he focused on the road. His dark eyes burned into hers. Heat warmed her cheeks, and the soft flesh at the base of her neck tingled.

"Rocky feels hot," she said, raising her voice to be heard over the sound of the motor. "He can't travel far."

Sanchez turned and glanced down at Robbie. "We'll stop soon."

Maybe he had an ounce of decency hidden under all that anger after all. She grasped her brother's hand and squeezed, hoping he could feel the encouragement and support in her touch.

Through the window, she saw the Atlanta skyline to her left. The golden dome of the State Capitol was visible in the distance. The turnoff for the Interstate 75-85 connector lay ahead.

Chilled from the cold, she wrapped her arms around her chest. As if sensing her discomfort, Joe reached for the heater. A blast of warm air blew from the overhead duct.

Arnie mumbled something from the front seat, and Joe switched lanes. If they exited downtown, they'd be caught in the holiday parade. Crowds of people lined Peachtree Street and International Boulevard.

Gridlock might provide the opportunity to escape. Once the van stopped, she could throw the door open and scream for help.

A surge of hope filled her. She inched toward the door. Joe turned onto the connector, heading north. Three exits until International Boulevard and the throng of holiday merrymakers. Not that she wanted anyone else to be hurt.

A cell chirped from the front of the van.

Arnie fumbled for the phone and pulled it to his ear. "Yeah?"

He grumbled. "Right." Flipping his cell closed, he glanced back at Sanchez and Malachi. "Streets downtown are closed." He reached for the radio knob.

Christmas music piped through the speakers: "Peace on earth, goodwill to men…"

Peace? Goodwill? The three gunmen, holding them hostage, had an opposing point of view.

Once again, her gaze settled on Joe. Did he believe in peace on earth, or had he been warped by the crime and depravity with which he came into contact in his line of work? Hard to be optimistic about man's nature when all he saw was the underbelly of society.

What had happened to the world? Callie sighed, their situation heavy on her heart. Joe looked at her in the mirror as if he understood her frustration and upset. Despite the odds, she felt a wave of confidence sweep over her.

The Christmas song ended.

"This just in." The radio announcer's voice cut over the hum of the motor and the sound of the wheels spinning along the asphalt. "A shoot-out at a local nursing home has left an officer and the facility's head nurse severely injured. Police were unable to question the wounded, but the gunman involved with the local gang, the Exterminators, has been kidnapped. Police have set up roadblocks to all routes leaving the city. The group is armed and dangerous, and citizens are asked to notify police if they see anything suspicious."

Arnie clicked the radio off. "Leave the connector at the next exit."

Joe steered the van into the right lane and decelerated onto the ramp. Callie's heart plummeted. They were heading east, away from the parade route.

Arnie turned to catch her eye. "You live close by?"

"Not far," she said, wondering if he planned to hole up at her apartment. She thought of the elderly gentleman who sat by his window and watched everyone's comings and goings. If anything seemed amiss, he'd knock on her door to check on her. Another neighbor, a sweet widow, had promised to bring over a plate of holiday cookies this afternoon.

Callie couldn't let them be brought into this situation, yet riding in the back of the utility van wasn't good for Robbie. He needed bed rest and time to heal. For her own peace of mind, she wanted to run the lab tests that would tell how his condition was progressing.

She adjusted the blanket around Robbie and pulled her hand back, noticing blood on her fingers. Tugging the blanket and hospital gown aside, she saw the bright red stain on the gauze dressing, covering his incision. Robbie needed to be stabilized to stop the bleeding. A complete blood count, or CBC, would determine the amount of blood he had already lost.

"Magnolia Medical isn't far from here," she blurted out before she could weigh her words.

The three gunmen turned and stared at her. Joe shot her a cold glance from the mirror.

"The main lab's closed over the holiday weekend," she explained. "No one will think to look for us there. We can park the van behind the building and out of sight. I'll be able to run Rocky's lab tests. There are medical supplies, blood for transfusion."

Arnie snorted. "I don't like labs."

"Rocky's bleeding bad," Sanchez confirmed, gazing at the stained bandage.

"All right, all right." The ringleader nodded. "We'll hole up at Magnolia Medical."

Joe turned left at the next intersection and headed for the large medical complex situated on the edge of town. The cop looked back, his eyes hooded.

Callie's heart quickened, realizing too late she had provided the gunmen exactly what they needed—a safe place to hide out.

Her stomach dropped. What had she done? Reacting too quickly, she'd provided the gunmen with the perfect solution to their problem—a problem that had just grown worse for Callie, her brother and the driver, whose neck muscles were already tensed with frustration.

She touched Robbie's side as fresh blood stained the gauze. If only she'd learned when to keep her mouth shut.

Long ago, she'd suggested her sister play outside. Callie had made a mistake then that had led to her sister's death. Hopefully, she hadn't made a second mistake that would cost her brother's life, as well.

Chapter Five

Joe gripped the steering wheel, trying to override the frustration that was bubbling up within him. Cute as she was, Callie had a stubborn determination that might get them all killed. Most folks would be cowering back in silence, afraid to mumble a word. Not this gal. She was becoming more vocal by the minute.

"Turn left at the next intersection," Arnie directed. Driving away from the busy downtown, Joe steered the van through an industrial area. Empty parking lots signaled plant employees had the Christmas weekend off. No one would notice the van snaking along this deserted back road toward the laboratory.

In the distance, Joe saw the top of the Magnolia Medical complex above the barren treetops. A few doctor's offices and small medical clinics bordered the side roads. A drugstore appeared to be the only place open for business. A couple of cars were parked out front.

Arnie grunted for Joe to turn into the laboratory lot and steer toward the rear of the main building, where the parked van would appear to be waiting for employees, returning to work on Monday morning. If this situation wasn't resolved by then, the medical personnel going into the lab would be put in danger, as well.

Following Arnie's direction, Joe parked near a side entrance. Sanchez climbed out and opened the driver's door, his gun trained on Joe as he stepped to the pavement.

"Get the kid," Arnie ordered.

Rounding the van, Malachi opened the rear door. Joe held out his hands and helped Callie climb out. A scent as fresh as sunshine swirled around her, so different from the smell of death that clung to the gunmen.

He squeezed her fingers. "Are you okay?" Standing close, he could see her long lashes, which fluttered over her cheeks, the curve of her lips, the arch of her brow. His breath caught, and for an instant he thought only of how smooth Callie's skin felt to his touch.

"Move it," Arnie barked.

As she stepped aside, Joe glanced into

the van, seeing the kid's pain-stretched face wedged between the plastic containers. A small, clear area had provided Callie room to kneel at his side, which must have been uncomfortable for her as well, yet she hadn't complained.

Sensing her gaze, Joe turned. She stood next to Malachi, arms wrapped around her chest for warmth or to ward off the dread that lined her pretty face. Joe raised his chin, hoping she'd see the gesture as acknowledgment of her courage.

Wind swirled through the parking lot, scattering the last of the autumn leaves like lost souls looking for a place to rest. Joe quickly studied the surrounding area. Nothing indicated a source of help. Callie's words echoed in his mind: "No one will find us here."

Arnie dropped the bundle of keys he'd pulled from the ignition into Callie's hand and pushed her toward the side entrance. "Open the door," he ordered.

Joe lifted Rocky into his arms, and the kid's head rolled back. His eyelids fluttered but failed to open. Trying to keep him steady, Joe followed Arnie and Callie into the first floor of the laboratory's main building.

The ringleader shoved Callie along the corridor. She stumbled forward then caught herself and straightened. He grabbed her arm, but she jerked free.

Glancing right, then left, Joe familiarized himself with the building. Biohazard signs hung on various doors that undoubtedly led to labs off a central main corridor. He noticed a stairway at each end of the hallway. Water fountain. Public restrooms.

"The therapeutic donor room is on the third floor." Callie glanced back at the patient. "He'll be comfortable there."

She stopped at a bank of elevators and pushed the up button. The door whooshed open. They filed in, wearing strained expressions on their faces, and rode in silence to the third floor. The only sound was the kid's heavy breathing.

"This way." Callie took the lead when the elevator stopped. The lab was her home turf, and she walked with determined steps as if taking charge of the situation.

All that assertiveness could get her into trouble. Arnie Frazier wasn't known as a nice guy. He'd hurt anyone, including a woman, who didn't follow his directions.

Callie opened a steel door, which bore an Authorized Personnel Only sign and a biohazard logo. The smell of chemicals wafted past Joe, sharp, acidic, not totally unpleasant but distinctive in an antiseptic way. He followed Arnie across the threshold and into an expansive clinical lab. Rows of slate countertops and overhanging cabinets filled with laboratory supplies occupied the greater portion of the room.

The ringleader hesitated. "This place filled with germs?"

"Depends. Watch where you put your hands." Callie kept moving past a number of freestanding automated analyzers and a row of refrigerators.

Arnie caught Sanchez's eye and motioned him forward. "Check it out. Make sure no one's around to disrupt our privacy. Cut the phone lines while you're at it."

Sanchez grunted and headed off on his own.

Joe spied a smaller room to the right. The sign above the door read Micro Lab.

"In here." Callie pointed them forward. A fire extinguisher hung on the wall behind her.

Still carrying the kid, Joe stepped into the windowless room about the size of a two-car garage. Four padded contoured donor chairs sat two-by-two in the center. The walls were edged with the same slate counters and over-hanging cabinets as in the main lab area.

A small Christmas tree stood dark in the corner. On the nearby countertop, ceramic figures of Joseph and Mary huddled around a tiny infant in what appeared to be a hand-made stable.

"You draw units of blood in here?" Arnie asked as he looked around.

"Not the blood used for transfusions," Callie explained. "This room is for patients who have hemochromatosis—too much iron in their blood. Every so often they need a unit drawn off to drop their levels into normal range."

Arnie nodded as if he understood about iron levels and therapeutic blood draws. Opening a door on the far side of the room, he peered into the corridor at the stairwell directly opposite. Evidently satisfied, he closed the door.

Callie pulled a bedsheet from the wall cabinet and slipped it over the leather recliner then helped Joe lower Robbie onto the chair, his hips angled into the contour. Pushing aside the hospital gown, she checked the blood-tinged gauze that covered the incision on his side before she drew a blanket from another cabinet, covered him and tucked the fabric under his legs.

Joe walked to the sink, searching for something—anything—that could serve as a weapon.

Malachi raised his gun. "Whatta think you're doing?"

"Washing my hands." Joe turned on the water and lathered his hands with soap. "I need to examine your buddy."

Lowering his weapon, the mocha-skinned gunman leaned against the counter and shrugged. "Watch your step."

Once Joe dried his hands, he reached for the latex gloves on the counter and held the box out to Arnie, who stood with his back against the wall.

The gunman hesitated for a moment then pulled out two gloves and slipped them over his hands. Evidently he didn't like germs.

Callie handed Joe a disposable lab coat and held another one out for Arnie. He shrugged off the offer.

"Doing okay?" Joe whispered, his voice muffled by the running water as she washed her hands.

"Scared."

The tremble of fear he heard in her voice cut into his heart.

"Anyone expecting you home today?"

She shook her head.

"What about at Lazarus House? Won't someone realize you were working today?"

"I got a call about an hour ago. I visit the patients most weekends. I was asked if I could fill in by drawing some of the lab work."

"So no one would suspect you've been taken hostage?"

Once again she shook her head. Joe didn't want to sound an alarm, but it seemed neither he nor Callie would be missed by anyone today. From the news report, he knew the cops hadn't been able to question the guard or head nurse, so the responsibility of escaping rested solely on Joe's shoulders.

"Stay out of their way and keep quiet," he told her. "Let me handle the gunmen."

Their gazes locked. Her eyes were clear as a mountain stream.

Wanting to focus on something other than Callie Evans, he glanced at the supply cabinet in the corner. "I need a weapon. A scalpel, scissors. Anything sharp that can inflict a wound."

Sanchez returned to the donor room. "The lab checks out, Arnie." He caught sight of the wall phone hanging in the corner. "You want me to cut that phone line, too?"

The ringleader shook his head. "Leave it. We might need it later."

Spying the reclining chairs, Sanchez smiled. "I'm gonna stretch out and relax for a while." He holstered his weapon and pointed to a wall-mounted television. "How 'bout turning on the tube?"

Malachi raised his hand and flipped the power switch. A Spanish variety show came on. The sounds of Christmas carols—some sung in English, some in Spanish—filled the room.

"Help me out when I examine the patient," Joe whispered as he slipped into the lab coat and gloves then stepped to the donor chair where Robbie lay.

Noticing how Arnie was staring at them, Callie raised her voice for his benefit as she pulled on gloves. "I'll draw the CBC you ordered and the chemistry panel."

"Perfect." Joe took the kid's pulse then checked the whites of his eyes, felt the lymph glands on his neck and palpitated his lower abdomen. At least he knew the basics. Hopefully his act would convince the gunmen he was a qualified physician.

Callie pulled a stethoscope from the cabinet drawer. Wrapping the cuff around the kid's upper arm, she pumped up the pressure and watched the indicator slowly drop. "One hundred over seventy-five."

"We need to keep him stable so his blood pressure doesn't drop," Joe said.

Callie pulled the blood-drawing supplies she'd grabbed at Lazarus House from her pocket. Tying a tourniquet around the patient's arm, she swabbed his vein and inserted the needle. Joe glanced over his shoulder at Arnie. The gunman's face blanched, and he averted his gaze as the color-coded tubes filled with blood.

Working swiftly, Callie unsnapped the tourniquet and jabbed a gauze square against the point of entry before discarding the needle into the special receptacle for sharp objects hanging on the wall.

The kid's eyes fluttered open. "Cal…?"

Sanchez stared at the television. Malachi asked a question that deflected the ringleader's attention. Turning back to the patient, Joe leaned down. "What is it, kid?"

Still dehydrated from surgery, he tried to swallow. "Cal…?"

Callie grabbed his hand. "I'm here, Robbie."

His lips broke into a strained smile. "Callie," he whispered, and then his eyes closed, and he slipped back to sleep.

A sinking feeling settled in the pit of Joe's stomach. "You know the kid?"

Face drawn, she pulled back ever so slightly. "He...he's my brother."

The air knocked out of Joe's lungs. Callie and the kid were related? Now *that* was a complication he hadn't expected.

Up to this point, Callie had trusted him, but that might change if she found out the truth. Joe had ordered the middle-of-the-night transfer to Lazarus House to keep Robbie out of the hands of the Exterminators. Unfortunately, his strategy had backfired.

As much as he wanted to explain everything to Callie, he couldn't. The stakes were too high, and emotions were stretched too thin. It was easy to see how much she loved her brother. If anything happened to him, she would never forgive Joe. Even though they'd been together only a short time, he wanted to ensure their fragile relationship stayed intact.

His job was to get her out alive.

Maybe then he would be able to share the secret Robbie's sister needed to know.

Chapter Six

Working as efficiently as possible under the trying conditions, Callie smoothed the blanket over Robbie and tucked the edges under his legs. When her hand brushed his calf, he jerked and groaned with pain.

Alarmed, she pulled back the blanket. The side of his leg was scraped. Normally, she wouldn't be concerned, but a small open sore, no larger than a dime, had erupted in the center of the irritated skin. A circle of angry, red tissue surrounded the opening, indicating infection. Something Robbie didn't need.

Callie grabbed a transfer tube and culture swabs from a nearby cabinet and rubbed them against the wound while Joe held Robbie's leg in place.

Arnie stepped out of the room. Despite his

tough-guy facade, he apparently had a problem with body fluids and open sores.

"How long will it take to know what's causing the infection?" Joe whispered. At least he understood the seriousness of this new complication.

"Depends how fast the organism grows. I'll make a smear and look at it under the microscope. If we're lucky, it may give me a clue about what bug we're dealing with. A more definite identification comes once the culture grows out, which could take twenty-four to forty-eight hours." Time they didn't have.

Lowering her voice, she added, "I've got scissors in the micro lab. I'll get them when I set up the culture."

Once she covered the sore with a gauze square, Joe helped her smooth the blanket back into place.

His fingers touched hers. "Be careful, Callie."

Warmth spread through her and a sense of gratitude for the concern she saw in Joe's dark eyes. His calm in the face of crisis reassured her. Somehow he'd get them out of here.

She thought back to all the times she and Theo had prayed for his cop brother. God must have a sense of humor to allow Callie and Joe to meet under such trying circumstances.

Her daily prayer for so long had been for the Lord to bring Joe back into Theo's life. Either Joe or God had missed the mark at the nursing home by three rooms. She almost smiled, knowing the cop had been the one with the bad aim.

If the hostage situation ended on a positive note, she would do everything in her power to ensure the two brothers reconnected. Reconciliation might be asking too much, but God worked in mysterious ways, and His timing was perfect. Maybe He would even use their present predicament to bring about change for the better.

"Theo was right," she said, seeing confusion wrap around Joe's handsome face. "Your brother said you were a good man."

An edge of vulnerability flashed in Joe's eyes. There was a lot of hurt in his past, Callie knew. Every family had problems. Some more than most. Her own proved the point.

She'd made a mistake the last time she and Robbie had been together. This time she'd ensure her brother knew she loved him. She'd let him know the Lord loved him as well. From what Theo had said, Joe might need that same message.

Malachi peered down at the patient. "How's he doing?"

"Rocky needs to be in a hospital," Joe insisted.

"Forget it." Arnie stepped back into the donor room, appearing somewhat composed now that the wound was covered.

Callie gathered the tubes of blood and culture swabs. "I need to run these lab tests."

"Malachi, go with her." Arnie pointed Joe to the corner. "Sit on the floor, Doc."

"If I help her, we'll have the results faster," Joe said.

"Malachi, aim your gun at her head. One wrong move and she dies." Arnie glared at Joe. "Got it?"

He fisted his hands. "Yeah, I've got it."

Callie sent him a reassuring glance, hoping he got the message. She'd be okay as long as he didn't do anything rash.

Malachi followed her into the small microbiology lab and plopped down on one of the tall swivel chairs.

Callie pulled in a calming breath, hoping to ease some of the tension that tightened the muscles in her neck. She labeled three petri dishes then touched the end of the cotton swab, containing the discharge from the sore on Robbie's leg, to the gel culture media. Lighting a Bunsen burner, she sterilized a tiny steel loop in the flame and streaked the discharge across each plate.

When Callie opened a drawer under the work area, she spied the scissors Joe needed. Turning ever so slightly, she found Malachi staring at her.

"Something wrong?" he asked.

"No, of course not." She pulled a microscope slide from the drawer. Callie rubbed the swab over the glass and allowed it to air-dry before she placed it onto the automatic staining machine.

As the slide dropped into position and was covered with the first of a series of dyes, Callie returned the plates to the incubators. As attentive as Malachi was, she'd have to come back later for the scissors.

Motioning for him to follow her into the main laboratory area, she headed for the chemistry analyzers. As she prepared her brother's blood specimen for testing, Malachi leaned back against the slate countertop. The tension in his face eased. Away from Arnie, he seemed to let down his guard.

"You from around here?" she asked, hoping to develop a rapport with the youngest gunman.

He nodded. "Decatur's home. My mama and grandma live there."

"Bet they'd like to see you on Christmas."

"Yeah. There's a big family get-together. My mama's been cooking all week."

"Turkey and dressing?"

He nodded and smiled. "Corn-bread stuffing, collard greens, sweet-potato-and-pecan pie." Malachi swallowed as if tasting the holiday treats, his eyes wistful. "My mama's gonna be disappointed if I'm not there for supper."

"Ask Arnie. Maybe he'll let you leave."

The gunman straightened. Perhaps she'd said too much.

Callie programmed the tests into the analyzer before she spoke again. "Smart guy like you could make a difference in the world. Ever think of going straight?"

He shrugged. "My mama said I should be a preacher."

Callie almost dropped the tube of blood she held. Either Malachi's mother didn't know the depth of his gang involvement or she had extraordinary confidence in God's redeeming love to change her son's heart.

"Sounds like your mama wants you to be right with the Lord."

"I believed when I was a kid. Don't have time for God no more. Gotta job to do. Gotta stay strong, you know what I mean?"

Evidently Malachi had a flawed view of what it meant to be a Christian. "So you think believing in God would make you less of a man?"

"I'm just sayin' I've got other things to do."

"Like holding people hostage?" she asked.

He stiffened. "We didn't start out to do anybody no harm. Just needed to get Rocky. Make sure he was safe."

Robbie would have been safer remaining at Lazarus House, but Callie doubted the gunman would agree. "He needs medical care."

Malachi waved his arms in the air. "But you've got all these medical machines to make him better right here." He pointed a finger at her chest. "You're a nurse. The doc's with him now."

"I'm a medical technologist," she corrected. And the doc's a cop. A fact she wouldn't mention. "The tests will determine the seriousness of Rocky's condition, but he needs intensive care that he can only get at a hospital."

"He wasn't in a hospital when we grabbed him. He was in an old folks' home."

"Lazarus House is a long-term nursing facility where he had full-time care," Callie explained.

"But they moved him there from Grady, the biggest hospital in the city."

Malachi was right. Under the cops' insistence, no doubt. Tamika had said the transfer was in response to information law enforcement had received about the Exterminators.

Callie would like to meet the wise guy who suggested her brother would be safe at the residential care facility. She'd give him a piece of her mind. He'd made a mistake—a big mistake that could cost three people their lives.

Once the chemistry analyzer was running, Callie focused on the CBC. The results confirmed that Robbie's red blood count was low. Any additional loss of blood would be life threatening.

Conversely, his white blood count was elevated, indicating a possible infection. Callie turned back to the chemistry analyzer as the results flashed across the monitor. She printed off a hard copy of all the tests and shoved them into Malachi's hand.

"Take these to the doc while I see if the

slide's finished staining." She motioned him into the donor room, relieved when Malachi complied with her request.

Slipping into the small side lab, Callie grabbed the scissors and shoved them into the pocket of her lab coat just as the young gunman stepped back into the room.

"Arnie wondered what's keeping you," he said.

"I'll be there in a minute." She extracted the now-stained slide from the drying rack, added a drop of immersion oil and placed it on the microscope. Cells swarmed into focus. She pulled her eyes away and invited Malachi over.

"Take a look," she said.

He leaned down to peer through the ocular, his gun close to her hand. Callie edged closer. Her fingers touched the cold metal.

Malachi jerked his head up, and his right hand went for the gun.

She pulled back just in time, keeping her gaze neutral. Inside she was shaking. "Did you see bacteria?"

Malachi stared at her for a long moment then nodded.

Callie kept talking, hoping to distract Malachi. "Bacteria with a circular shape are called cocci. It they appear in a chain, they're called streptococci."

Footsteps sounded at the doorway, and Sanchez stuck his head into the room. "Arnie wants to know if there's a problem."

"She's almost finished," Malachi said.

The Latino narrowed his eyes at Callie. "The doc's explaining the test results to Arnie. He wants to hear what you have to say."

Butterflies fluttered through Callie's stomach. If she contradicted Joe's assessment, the gunmen would realize one of them was a fraud.

Malachi grabbed her arm and shoved her toward the door, suddenly needing to assert his authority. Callie would let him save face in front of Sanchez. For all Malachi's attempt to be tough, he had been raised by a God-fearing woman. Surely some of her prayers had rubbed off on her son.

The Christmas message could move the hardest heart. Maybe it could allow the youngest gunman to realize the error of his ways. Callie stepped back into the lab and glanced at her brother. If only his heart could change, as well.

She turned to Joe, their eyes locking. Once again, a sense of hope flowed over her, along with the confidence that God had brought them together for a purpose.

Arnie shoved the lab sheets into her face. "Tell me what these numbers mean."

Keep it simple, an inner voice cautioned. Callie knew that even if she provided a very basic overview of her brother's condition, without medical training, Joe would be hard-pressed to do the same. Providing contradictory information could prove fatal.

She took the papers and swallowed the fear that struggled to overpower her. Arnie aimed his gun at Joe's temple. The cop never blinked but continued to stare at her. His lips curved into a confident grin that made her pulse race and her frustration bubble anew. Why'd he always have to be so sure of himself?

"Come on, Callie," Arnie sneered. "Tell us what we need to know."

Chapter Seven

Joe wished he could reassure Callie. Trust your instincts, he'd tell her if he could. Arnie questioned Joe's medical expertise. Hopefully, the information Callie provided would wipe out any doubts the gunmen still harbored.

"Go on," Arnie insisted.

Callie swallowed. "Rocky's dehydrated, and he's lost blood. He has a scrape on his leg, which is infected. I saw a number of organisms present under the microscope that could produce a serious complication."

"As I told you, Arnie, your man needs IV antibiotic therapy as well as hydration," Joe said, confirming Callie's findings. "We're watching the wound on his chest. If he loses much more blood, he'll need a transfusion, as well."

Arnie grunted. "Rocky stays here. There are

two of you and one of him. Keep him alive."
He waved the gun between them. "If he dies,
you will, too."

A smirk crossed his face as he glared at Joe.
"I'm a gentleman, Doc. Ladies first."

Joe wanted to grab Arnie and squash him
like a bug, but he needed to do things by the
book. Let the rule of law deal with him. Fact
was, Arnie Frazier deserved solitary confinement for the rest of his life. Forget parole.

Unfortunately, with a .45 waving in the
air, Joe had to ignore Arnie's cocky rhetoric
and try to be a voice of reason in the midst of
chaos.

Stepping around the gunman, Joe moved
back to the patient's side. "Callie, if you'll help
me, we'll check his leg again."

Worry pulled at her pretty face, but she appeared to muster an inner strength as she followed Joe's lead.

Malachi approached Arnie. "Hey, man, it's
Christmas Eve. Maybe we should split up tomorrow."

Sanchez moved closer. "I told my wife and
kids I'd be in Juarez late Christmas night."

"I'm in charge," Arnie scoffed. "We stay
here until I say otherwise."

"Ah, man," Malachi groused.

Sanchez muttered something in Spanish.

While the gunmen bickered, Callie whispered to Joe. "What did you tell Arnie about the lab test results?"

"The same thing you said."

She looked up. "But how did you know what the test results meant?"

"EMT training while I was in the military. Basic medical triage. Nothing sophisticated or high tech. Evidently, it was enough to satisfy Arnie."

"Thank you, God," Callie whispered.

"While you're sending up that thank-you, better ask Him how we can get antibiotics for your brother."

"There's a drugstore not far from here. Arnie might let me get a prescription filled."

Joe remembered seeing the pharmacy earlier.

"Our lab pathologist keeps a prescription pad in his office," Callie continued. "I'll write the order for an antibiotic and pain medicine. You'll need to sign his name."

"Arnie won't let you out of here alone."

"I'll see if Malachi can go with me. He's not as hard-hearted as he likes to pretend."

"If you can get away from him, call the

cops. Tell them where we are. They'll send in a SWAT team."

She slipped her hand into her lab coat pocket. "I got the scissors."

"You're amazing." He smiled. Callie *was* amazing. She was strong and determined and resourceful. Hopefully, she'd find a way to get away from Malachi.

Joe shoved the scissors into the pocket of his sweatpants, comforted to know he had a weapon. He'd wait until she left the lab before he executed his next move. Hopefully one that would end the hostage situation once and for all.

Together, he and Callie checked the kid's blood pressure. Still low.

"How bad is it?" Arnie asked from across the room.

"He needs an antibiotic and pain medicine," Joe insisted. "If I write a prescription, you can send one of your goons with Callie to get it filled at the nearby pharmacy."

"The prescription pad is in the lab office. I'll get it." She started for the main lab.

Arnie glared at Malachi. "Go with her. Don't let her out of your sight."

As the two left the room, Sanchez adjusted

the volume on the television and lowered himself onto the donor chair.

Joe checked Robbie's side. The bleeding had eased. He pulled back the sheet that covered his leg. The skin around the scrape appeared swollen and hot, worse than when Joe had first seen the gash just a short while ago.

Callie returned with the pad and ballpoint pen. "I wrote the prescriptions as you told me to do," she said for the gunmen's benefit. "A broad-spectrum antibiotic and high-dose pain-killer." She had also traced the pathologist's signature lightly in pencil to guide Joe's hand.

Arnie and Malachi continued to argue about when to leave Magnolia Medical. Malachi was determined to have Christmas dinner with his mother and family. Arnie seemed increasingly aggravated with the tall, lanky gunman's plans for Christmas Day.

"Remember, Callie, get away from Malachi as soon as you can," Joe whispered. "Call the police. Tell them about the stairway that leads to the back hallway. The phone's still connected in this room. Tell them to call and let the phone ring twice to warn me they're ready to charge the lab. I'll distract the gunmen until they arrive."

She nodded, her eyes wide, but she showed

no sign of fear. He admired her courage and hated putting her in danger.

Once he signed the prescriptions, she turned to Malachi. "Are you ready?"

Arnie held up his hand. "Not so fast." The ringleader nudged Sanchez. "You go with her. Take the van. If she tries anything, shoot first, ask questions later."

Joe's gut tightened. Callie had developed a rapport with Malachi and had a better chance of getting away from him. Sanchez wouldn't let down his guard even for a second.

Sanchez grabbed Callie's upper arm and shoved her toward the door. "Let's go, doll."

She glanced over her shoulder at her brother then raised her eyes to Joe. He nodded with encouragement, feeling the weight of the scissors in his pocket.

"Get her out alive," Joe mumbled, wondering to whom he was addressing the request. Certainly not God. With his track record, the Almighty would never answer Joe's prayer for help.

Sanchez's fingers were tight on Callie's arm. As hard as she tried, she couldn't jerk free from his grasp. Joe was counting on her, but she wasn't sure she could do anything heroic. Hopefully, the pharmacist—a man she knew—would recognize the forged signature and come to her aid.

Callie remained optimistic until she and Sanchez walked into the drugstore. Within a few seconds, she realized the pharmacist was preoccupied with a cute blonde who seemed to strike his fancy as she waited for her prescription. With his focus on the woman instead of his work, the pharmacist overlooked the incorrect answers Callie gave to some of his questions as well as the *Call Police* message she wrote instead of her signature at the bottom of the credit card sales receipt. He shoved the slip of paper into the bottom drawer of his cash register without noticing her cryptic plea for help.

Sanchez hovered close by, his weapon aimed at her from the pocket of his jacket. Children scurried through the store dangerously close to the Latino gunman and his weapon. As much as Callie needed to get help, she couldn't do anything that would endanger the little ones.

Her heart plummeted as they left the store and climbed into the Magnolia Medical van. She had the medication Robbie needed, but she hadn't been able to warn anyone about what was happening at Magnolia Medical, nor had she been able to get free from Sanchez.

"Grab the drugs," he ordered when they parked in the rear of the laboratory. He yanked the keys from the ignition and held the gun on her as they both dropped to the pavement.

When he rounded the front of the van, she took off running, her eyes focused on the wooded area at the far end of the parking lot.

Sanchez cursed and raced after her, his footfalls slamming against the concrete. "Stop or I'll shoot," he shouted.

He could kill her as easily inside the lab as out here. Callie had to get away. The muscles in her legs burned, and she gasped for air, feeling tightness in her chest.

Sanchez's labored breathing sounded in her ear. He was gaining. Calling on an inner strength, she increased her pace. Twenty feet more and she'd enter the wooded area surrounding the lab complex. A small gate would take her out of the fenced compound. Fifty yards beyond that she could see a gas station, where help hopefully waited.

His hand grabbed her shoulder. She screamed and stumbled to the pavement. Her knees scraped against the cement, ripping her skin open. Gravel cut the palms of her hands when she tried to break her fall.

Sanchez wove his fingers through her hair and pulled her to her feet. Callie cried out in pain. Hot tears stung her eyes. She'd failed. Joe was counting on her. Robbie wouldn't last much longer. Their survival depended on Callie, and she'd let them down.

Oh, God, I'm so sorry, she moaned. Sanchez shoved her toward the lab. If the gunmen killed Joe or Robbie, their deaths would rest on her shoulders. Right now, the thought of losing them and the guilt she would carry was too much for her to bear.

Joe knew everything would happen fast once Callie contacted the police. The two-ring hang-up phone call would signal that the SWAT team was in place and ready to storm the lab.

His plan was straightforward. He'd attack Arnie with the scissors before Malachi went for his gun. Caught off guard, the gunmen would be overpowered once the SWAT team stepped through the door.

Relieved that Callie wouldn't be in the middle of the milieu, Joe's heart warmed thinking of her courage. Hopefully she'd gotten free from Sanchez.

Malachi lounged on the chair Sanchez had vacated and watched an old rerun of a classic Christmas movie. Arnie's eyes were heavy as he glanced between the overhead screen and the floor where Joe sat. Robbie moaned occasionally and called out twice in pain.

The phone rang sooner than Joe had expected, and before he could dig the scissors from his pocket. Callie must have gotten away from Sanchez immediately after leaving the lab. Both gunmen looked up, but neither made an attempt to answer the phone.

"Want me to get that?" Joe stood and stretched.

"Sit down," Arnie demanded.

"I need to use the restroom."

The ringleader nodded to Malachi. "Take him to the men's room. Watch him."

Malachi's eyes were fixed on the TV. He laughed at something one of the characters said as he slid off the chair.

Arnie glanced at the screen, giving Joe the chance he needed.

He lunged for the weapon jammed in Malachi's waistband. Taken off guard, the lanky Exterminator fell back against the donor chair. His gun clattered to the floor.

Joe slammed his fist into Malachi's jaw. Stunned, he tried to stand as Joe bent to retrieve the handgun.

"Back off," Arnie yelled.

Ignoring the warning and unable to grab the dropped weapon, Joe jabbed his shoulder into Malachi's gut. The gunman's fingers circled Joe's neck, constricting his airway.

He gasped and pulled the scissors from his pocket.

Arnie raised his weapon. Instinctively, Joe shifted, pulling Malachi off balance.

In that split second the gun went off, the sound deafening.

Joe sucked in a lungful of air, expecting pain. Instead, Malachi slumped to the floor, a gapping wound to his side. His face twisted. He stretched a hand out to Arnie. "Why... why'd you shoot me, man?"

Arnie stared at him as if dazed, his mouth open, eyes wide.

Spying Malachi's gun under the donor chair, Joe dropped to his knees and reached for the weapon.

"No," Arnie screamed. He fired again.

Pain sliced though Joe's shoulder. The scissors dropped from his hand.

Arnie slammed the barrel of his gun into the base of Joe's neck.

He gasped and fell to the floor.

Where was the SWAT team?

The door to the lab opened. Relief spread over Joe.

He looked up, but instead of the well-trained team of law enforcement professionals, he saw Sanchez with his hand around Callie's neck.

Chapter Eight

"Oh, dear Lord, help us all," Callie cried, taking everything in as she entered the donor room. Her gaze flicked from her brother to Malachi to Joe, who struggled to rise off the floor.

The phone rang, the shrill sound echoing through the lab.

Sanchez released his hold on her, reached for the receiver and brought it to his ear.

"Yeah?" He shook his head. "You've got the wrong number, dude."

Callie raced to Joe's side.

"I'm okay," he whispered, his voice raspy.

"What happened?"

"Guess I was in the line of fire." His crooked smile pulled at her heart.

"Looks like you had a little problem," Sanchez said to Arnie.

"The doc got carried away."

"What about Malachi?"

"Lift him onto that reclining chair."

Sanchez's eyes were wide. "He's bleeding real bad, Arnie."

The older guy shrugged. "Shove a towel against his wound."

"There's one in the bottom drawer." Callie pointed to the metal cabinet.

Sanchez lifted the moaning gunman onto the chair. Opening the drawer, he grabbed a white terry-cloth towel and held it against the wound.

Callie pulled two plastic pill bottles from the shopping bag. Arnie grabbed them out of her hand. "Give me those. I say who gets the drugs and when."

"Rocky needs the antibiotic."

"He's asleep. Tend to Malachi first."

She wasn't a doctor, but she knew the wounded gunman's condition was critical. The bullet had entered his back and exited through his chest. Using the basic supplies on hand, she bandaged the wound. Robbie was sleeping, so she quickly moved back to help Joe.

"It's only a flesh wound," he said, trying to

make light of something that had to be painful. "I'll be okay, Callie."

"Would you stop with the macho male routine," she said under her breath. "Your wound needs to be cleaned."

Daring Arnie to stop her, she reached for the scissors where they lay on the floor. The way she felt, if he objected, he'd get a piece of her mind. She cut through the sleeve of Joe's shirt then placed the shears on the counter.

Arnie grunted as he shoved them into his back pocket and focused on the television. Sanchez stood against the wall, equally distracted.

Callie examined Joe's torn flesh. "Trying to take two men with a pair of scissors wasn't smart. Anyone ever tell you to think before you act?"

"You sound like you're angry."

"Peeved, not angry."

"Because I tried to get the upper hand?"

"The odds were against you, Joe."

"I had to do something."

She raised her gaze and realized too late that their lips were only inches apart. As much as she tried to focus on what he was saying, her mind kept thinking about the way his mouth twitched when he tried to smile and the hint of limey aftershave mixed with the smell of hardworking male that drew her like a moth to flame.

"Don't talk to me," she finally insisted.

"What?"

"You're distracting me."

Once again, his mouth curved into a cocky grin that sent her heart into arrhythmia. Wounded, outnumbered and still he had a magnetism that made her internal compass spin out of control.

"Close your eyes," she whispered.

"You gonna kiss me?" His voice was low and husky and stretched with tension that caused her inner thermostat to rise.

She opened a small first-aid kit. "I'm going to clean out your wound. It'll be easier for me if you don't watch."

"Yes, ma'am. But I'll be thinking of you."

His thick lashes dropped over his eyes, giving her time to examine his angular face. His cheek was swollen and a growth of beard darkened his jaw, which for some reason she suddenly wanted to touch. Instead, she turned back to his wound and cleaned the injured shoulder.

"Tell me when you're finished," he said.

"Almost done."

His eyes blinked open. "Thanks," he whispered, flashing a megawatt smile that sent a surge of static electricity dancing along her spine.

"I tried to get away," Callie said, needing to turn her mind to something other than the way he looked and smelled and how much she wanted to rub her hands over his injured shoulder.

"The pharmacist should have realized something was wrong," she said. "But he was looking at a pretty face and ignored my efforts to get his attention."

"A pretty face like yours?"

She touched the back of her hand to his forehead. "No fever yet, but you sound delusional."

"You are beautiful, Callie." He stole a glance at the two gunmen who seemed mesmerized by the television program before he turned his gaze back to her.

Raising his right hand, Joe touched her cheek. "Very, very beautiful."

For a second, the donor room, the gunmen, her injured brother—everything faded into darkness until she and Joe were the only people in the light.

Neither of them spoke. They didn't need to. For this split second in time, they were joined together. Their future, their destinies intertwined. Life or death? Everything depended on what happened next.

"We need a plan," Callie whispered when her heart had stilled enough for her to form a thought and express it in words.

Joe wrapped his fingers through hers. "Keep a low profile. I'll take care of everything."

"Which you keep saying, but from the looks of your shoulder, you're not my vote for most likely to succeed."

He smiled. "Straightforward, aren't you?"

"Determined to find a way out of this hostage situation. It's not how I want to spend Christmas."

"Why, that hurts my feelings." Playing along, he feigned a pout.

The guy was crazy. Crazy cute with an attitude that made her want to hug him, injured shoulder or not. "I can take care of myself, you know, Joe."

He rolled his eyes. "Yeah? What's that on your knee? Looks like you and Sanchez didn't see things eye to eye."

"I told you I tried to get away."

Suddenly, he became serious again. "Let me handle the bad guys. Okay, Callie? I'm trained at this."

A commercial came on the television. Arnie

motioned to her. "See what you can do for Malachi before he bleeds to death."

When Joe started to stand, the ringleader shook his head. "Stay where you are, Doc."

The towel shoved against Malachi's wound was soaked with blood. Callie changed the dressing then drew a few tubes of blood from Malachi's arm. The lab tests confirmed his red blood count was dangerously low.

"He needs a transfusion," she told Arnie.

Relieved when the ringleader allowed her to move unaccompanied into the blood bank without Sanchez, Callie quickly set up the crossmatch. Once completed, she hurried back to Malachi, a unit of blood in hand. Joe was sitting near the wounded gunman taking his pulse and blood pressure. Even with the bandaged shoulder and swollen eye, he looked professional in the lab coat and latex gloves. Her heart fluttered with the memory of their moment together.

Starting an IV wasn't in her job description, but she'd drawn enough blood to be able to hit the vein. Joe had EMT training, and between the two of them, they managed to get the job done. Luckily, the gunmen kept their eyes on the television instead of Joe and Callie's fumbling attempts to hang the unit of blood.

Once the life-giving blood was dripping into the gunman's arm, Arnie stepped closer.

"He needs a couple of those painkillers," Joe said. Arnie shook two caplets into Joe's hand.

"Sanchez." Arnie glared at the Latino. "Get a glass of water for Malachi."

"Get it yourself," Sanchez groused.

Arnie rested his hand on the gun jammed in his waistband.

Sanchez threw his hands in the air. "Okay, man. I'll get water. Next time, just ask pretty."

"You'll find bottled water in the employee break room." Callie pointed him in the right direction as she headed into the micro lab to check Robbie's culture.

She pulled the petri dishes from the incubator and removed the lids. The muscles in her back tightened. A faint clear halo surrounded the tiny clusters of bacteria overgrowing the plate.

Working quickly, she ran a few more tests.

"No," she moaned, when the results confirmed her suspicion.

Rushing back to the donor room, Callie jerked the blanket off her brother's leg. The scrape that had appeared red and swollen just a few hours earlier had tripled in size to a black hole of raw flesh. The surrounding skin had darkened and dried like seaweed on the outside of a sushi roll.

Joe stared at the blackened flesh.

Arnie spied the wound and backed toward the door.

"Callie?" Joe reached for her hand. "What is it?"

"A fast-acting bacteria. Necrotizing fasciitis is the medical term. You may have heard it called by another name."

Tears swelled in her eyes. She blinked to keep them in check but was unsuccessful. As they streamed down her cheeks, she shook her head.

"Robbie's infected with flesh-eating strep."

Even without medical training, Joe knew Robbie's condition had taken a drastic turn for the worse. "At least he's on an antibiotic."

"Oral antimicrobials won't work." Callie wiped her hand across her cheeks, drying the tears. "He needs IVs pumping through his body. Even the strongest antibiotics might not make a difference."

Sanchez moved closer. "How come you don't know that, Doc?" He glanced back at Arnie. "We got a problem with the medical guy. He's not up on his treatments."

Callie put her hands on her hips and glared at the Latino. "For your information, *Señor* Sanchez, physicians rely on medical technologists' expertise to help with diagnoses based on laboratory testing."

"Yeah? Whatever." He shrugged and returned to the donor chair.

Ignoring Sanchez, Joe moved to Robbie's side. "Callie, you'll have to assist me in caring for this wound."

She found a sterile debriding kit in the main lab and opened it for Joe.

"Guide me," he whispered, keeping his back to Arnie.

"I'm winging it, too." She handed him the round-tipped scissors. Using the tweezers, she lifted up an edge of the skin. "The dead flesh needs to be removed."

Joe rolled his eyes. "If you've got an in with someone upstairs, this might be the time to let Him know we could use help."

"I'll pray while you work." She paused then said, *"Dear Lord, help us. Help Robbie."*

Joe worked around the wound, relieved that Robbie seemed oblivious to what they were doing. Arnie stood in the doorway, arms crossed over his chest. A biohazard trash receptacle sat near his feet.

Once the necrotic skin had been removed, Callie dressed the wound with sterile gauze. Joe slipped the round-tipped scissors into his pocket and bundled the refuse into the towel and stepped toward the biohazard receptacle.

Arnie backed away. "What are you doing?"

Joe tossed the refuse in the special container. Unable to resist, he smirked at the gunman. "Just protecting you from germs."

The ringleader's face reddened. "I've had it with you, Doc." Arnie turned to Sanchez. "Tie him up."

"But—" Callie objected.

"Tie her up, too."

"I need my hands free to help Rocky and Malachi," Callie insisted.

Ignoring her request, Sanchez drew cable ties from his pocket. "I'll tie your hands in front so you can tend to the wounded. Okay, doll?"

Using a second tie, Sanchez bound Joe's wrists, taking pleasure in slapping his wounded shoulder when he was done.

Their chances of getting free had gone from bad to worse. Joe's shoulder ached, but his heart hurt more. He hadn't been able to protect Callie. Sanchez said they planned to kill the hostages before they left the lab, and the only weapon Joe had was a pair of debriding scissors he'd managed to slip into his pocket.

Chapter Nine

Joe sat next to Callie on the floor, their hands bound, their moods sober. She laid her head against his good shoulder and closed her eyes. More than anything, he wanted to wrap her in his arms and hold her tight. She had to be exhausted after working so hard to help her brother and care for Joe and Malachi. Before long, her breathing slipped into the gentle rhythm of sleep.

Sanchez lay on the donor chair, snoring. He, too, had succumbed to the long afternoon that had moved into an even longer night. The two other gunmen had done nothing except watch television and argue. Arnie had tuned to a variety show and seemed to enjoy the colorful costumes and larger-than-life theatrics. At some point in the afternoon, he'd grabbed a folding aluminum chair from the break room and now sat with his feet crossed at the ankles and his back against the wall.

With Callie sleeping next to him, Joe treasured the few minutes of quiet time he had with her. Eventually she sighed, and her eyes fluttered open. He shifted and tilted his head so his cheek touched her hair. The scent of her shampoo refreshed him like a spring rain.

"I'm sorry you had to be involved in this," he said.

"It's okay, Joe. Robbie is the one we need to worry about. His cheeks are flushed, and he has to be in a lot of pain. If only I could help him."

She shook her head. "Growing up, Robbie was a good kid. But now—?"

"Maybe you're jumping to the wrong conclusion."

"Oh, Joe, as much as the truth hurts, we're in this situation because of my brother. If he hadn't been working with the Exterminators, we wouldn't be held hostage."

Joe wished he could tell Callie the truth, but her brother's life and probably her own safety depended on the gunmen's need to get Robbie out of the city. If only Joe could find out who was running the operation. Once the head man was captured, law enforcement would be able to end the gang's corrupt hold on Atlanta.

"When was the last time you saw your brother?" Joe asked, hoping to learn a little more about their sibling relationship.

"He showed up at my door three years ago." She swallowed hard, as if the memory was painful. "We hadn't seen each other since our parents had divorced a number of years earlier. Our mother had died, and Robbie was grieving, which I didn't realize at the time. All I noticed was a twenty-one-year-old who had his hand out for money. When I said no, he paid me back by running up debt on my credit card."

"But you didn't press charges?"

She shook her head. "I couldn't. Jail wouldn't have been the answer. I told him I didn't want to see him again until he straightened out his life."

"Sounds like you were using tough love to help him," Joe volunteered.

"I wish my motive had been that honorable. When families break apart, there's a lot of pain. Kids feel responsible or caught in the middle. I hadn't gotten over my parents' divorce. For so long, I'd cried myself to sleep at night missing my dad, missing Robbie. I thought my mother was to blame for their breakup and was convinced Dad and Robbie felt the same."

She bit her lip. "According to my brother, I had it wrong. My dad hadn't missed me at all."

Tears sprang to her eyes, but she blinked them back, once again showing the strength Joe had seen throughout this hostage situation.

"Robbie's lucky to have you for a sister," he whispered. His lips brushed her hair.

Joe had longed for a strong relationship with his own brother. Unfortunately, all that had ended when his parents died.

Callie shook her head. "If Robbie had a caring sister, a sister who truly considered what the Lord wanted, my door would have stayed open for him. Instead I slammed it shut and warned him that unless he worked to improve his life, I wanted nothing to do with him."

"You were reacting to the pain you carried and to the way he'd tricked you. He expected you to save him when he really needed to save himself." Joe stared at the kid. "Something tells me he's learned his lesson."

Callie bit down on her upper lip. Her fingers caressed Joe's arm. His shoulder ached, but he didn't want to move for fear she'd pull away. Having Callie next to him made his world seem complete.

"What about Theo?" she finally asked. "He said you never forgave him."

Joe tensed. "My relationship with my brother is different."

"Is it?" She stared at him with a level gaze. The door to his past that had remained closed for so long opened ever so slightly.

Staring deep into her eyes, Joe knew Callie only saw the good in his brother. She didn't know about the other side of Theo.

"You expected Theo to take you in after your parents died," she said.

"Is that what he told you?"

"He told me he was twenty-one and living on his own. You thought he'd step into your dad's shoes, but Theo wasn't ready for that type of responsibility."

"You believed him, didn't you, Callie?"

"What I think isn't important. The real issue is what you think, Joe. Theo needs you."

He shook his head. "He didn't want me when I was a kid. Why would he want me in his life now?"

"He's all the family you have left, except for your foster parents. Theo said they're good people."

"Then that's one thing my brother and I agree on."

"He had his reasons for sending you to foster care, Joe."

"Did he tell you he was putting my needs first?" He bristled, angry that Theo convinced Callie he had done the right thing. There was nothing right about breaking a thirteen-year-old's heart.

Callie had bought into Theo's lies just as she'd bought into the lies about her own brother. Not that Joe had set her straight about Robbie. Did that make Joe the same as his brother?

The Petrecelli boys weren't known for the goodness in their hearts. They were known for making tough decisions. Sometimes they got it right. Sometimes they didn't.

He shifted his weight, trying to ease the pain that throbbed along his arm.

Sensing his discomfort, Callie called out to Arnie. "The doc needs a couple pain pills."

Joe started to shake his head no, but she nudged him. "Hush," she warned out of the corner of her mouth. "Let me handle this."

"I don't want medication."

"Got it. But I've got a plan."

Arnie pulled his focus from the television and stretched. "What do you want?"

"The doc's in a lot of pain. The pills might help him sleep."

Arnie snorted. "As much trouble as he's caused, might be good if he did sleep. One pill. He doesn't deserve to feel too good." He shook a caplet into Callie's outstretched hand.

"Would you mind handing me a bottle of water?" she asked.

Why'd she have to be so polite to the gunmen?

Arnie grabbed a bottle from the counter, and when he handed it to Callie, she looked imploringly up at him. "Arnie, would you mind cutting this tie so I can check on Rocky?"

Arnie grunted but cut the plastic that had bound her hands, freeing Callie to open the water bottle. Climbing to her knees, she held it up to Joe's lips. He drank deeply as Arnie returned to his chair.

"Now pretend you're taking the pill," she instructed, her voice a whisper.

Playing along, he took another large gulp of water.

"I gave Malachi one pill earlier and pocketed the other one. It could be useful to us later." Joe pulled a caplet from his pocket and dropped it into Callie's hand.

Arnie glanced back at the twosome, but she had already slipped both pills into her lab coat.

Leaving Joe and moving to her brother's side, Callie touched Robbie's forehead then eased the sheet aside.

Joe could see the wound had grown larger, killing more tissue as it ate through Robbie's flesh.

Her face whitened. Joe wanted to comfort her.

She turned to catch his eye and shook her head ever so slightly. He knew from the sorrow he saw in her expression and the sense of discouragement he read from her stance that the kid's condition had grown increasingly worse.

Joe needed to do something, but tied up, he didn't have many options. "Look, Arnie, I'll make a deal with you. Let Callie drive Rocky to the nearest hospital, and I'll stay with you as a hostage and do everything I can to get you out of the city. Without intensive IV antibiotic therapy, he won't survive."

"Yeah? Tell me how you can help."

"I'll drive the van. You and Sanchez hide in the back. The cops won't expect you to move on Christmas. They'll be understaffed with most of the guys at home, spending the holiday with their families."

Arnie rubbed his hand over his chin. "You've got a point."

Hopefully, the ringleader would buy into the hype. Truth was, many of the guys would have the day off, but departments throughout the greater metropolitan Atlanta area would still have adequate coverage to handle any emergency.

Once behind the wheel and with Callie and Robbie on their way to the hospital, Joe would do whatever was necessary to stop the two thugs. He wouldn't let Arnie and Sanchez get away.

Having overheard the conversation, Callie started toward the main laboratory. "There's a transport gurney in the histology department. I'll use it to take Rocky to my car. You take the lab van. If we all leave together, you'll be out of the city before I get to the hospital."

Sanchez's eyes blinked open. "What? We're leaving?" He raked his hand through his short hair.

Arnie grabbed Callie's arm, and she stopped and stared at him. "Is there a problem?" she asked.

Joe clenched his fist. The problem was Arnie. If only Joe could get the upper hand on that guy. Shoulder injury or not, he'd teach him a lesson about not touching Callie.

Arnie loosened his hold on her arm. "Get back to the corner."

"Rocky will die if he doesn't get to the hospital," she said.

"Let me worry about Rocky, okay?" Arnie said.

"What about Malachi?" Joe pushed. "He needs medical care as well."

"Shut up." Arnie wiped his hand over his jaw. "I need to think about what we're going to do."

If only he'd accept Joe's suggestion. Callie sighed as she dropped to the floor next to him. Her brother came first, and Joe knew she'd do whatever it took to get the medical care Robbie needed.

Arnie looked anything but concerned about either of the injured men and quickly turned his attention back to the television show. Despite his aversion to germs, he seemed to enjoy the entertainment and even laughed out loud a few times, a sound so opposite the feelings Joe harbored.

The night ahead would be difficult for everyone involved. Callie's discouragement, Robbie's wound that was eating at his flesh,

Malachi's breathing, which had grown more labored—there would be nothing merry about this Christmas Eve.

Callie wouldn't give up. She couldn't. Her whole life, she'd believed good triumphed over evil, even when her sister had died. As much as she hadn't understood what had happened or why, she knew God was a loving Father and didn't want suffering and despair for His children.

Resting her head on Joe's shoulder, she thought back to that other Christmas Day. Her mother had been getting the turkey out of the oven and would soon make the thick gravy that they'd spoon over the creamy mashed potatoes.

Her sister had been four, almost five. Rains had been heavy that December, and a morning shower had kept the children in the house. When the sun came out, Callie had asked if Becky could play in the fenced backyard.

"Make sure the gate is locked," had been her mother's only request.

From the back porch, Callie could see the gate was latched and too high for Becky's fingers to reach. Yet, fifteen minutes later, when her mother called the little girl for dinner, the backyard had been empty.

Callie closed her eyes, trying to block out the memory of her mother's screams and their frantic search. The police, the flashing lights, her sister's tiny body floating, facedown, in the nearby pond seemed too real even after all these years.

An accident, a gut-wrenching tragedy, cut their family in two. Callie never understood how her mother could turn on her father so mercilessly. He was grieving as much as any of them. Besides, her mother made it perfectly clear who was to blame.

"Forgive me, Lord," Callie whispered as she'd done a million times before. But nothing, not even the Lord's forgiveness, could absolve her of the guilt she carried.

Callie raised her eyes to her brother's feverish face. She'd been the reason one sibling had died. She couldn't let Robbie die on her watch, as well.

As if sensing her struggle, Joe nuzzled her with his cheek. "You okay, honey?"

She nodded. Having Joe's support made the pain of the past more bearable.

The closing credits for the show flashed on the television screen. Arnie stood and stretched. Sanchez rubbed his hand over his face. "Anything to eat around here?"

"There's some leftover food from the holiday potluck we had yesterday," she said. "I can fix a plate for everyone."

"Oh, Callie," Joe groaned. "I wish you'd stop trying to be so helpful."

She patted his arm. "Don't worry. I'll be okay."

As she stood, Arnie nodded to Sanchez. "Help her out. And like I said before, if she does anything strange, shoot first and ask questions later."

Stepping into the main lab, Callie looked back, catching Joe's eye from where he sat on the floor. With the wound to his shoulder and the infection in Robbie's leg getting worse, Callie had to act.

She just hoped Sanchez wouldn't get in the way. *Shoot first and ask questions later.* Arnie's words rumbled through her mind.

Oh, Lord, help me do the right thing.

Chapter Ten

Joe stood as Callie and Sanchez left the donor room. "Malachi needs another unit of blood."

"We'll wait for Callie." Arnie glared at him. "Sit."

Joe crumbled back to the floor. If he couldn't do anything else, he'd pump the ringleader for information that could be used later, once the hostage situation was over.

Joe had a sickening thought. Suppose the resolution didn't go the way he planned?

For an instant, he saw Callie's body lying on the floor. His stomach roiled from the mental picture that he forced from his mind. Attitude was half the battle. He had to stay focused on success.

"I heard someplace that the brains behind

the Exterminators is a big money tycoon from Atlanta."

Arnie sniffed. "You always so nosy?"

Ignoring the comment, Joe continued. "Some speculate the guy calling the shots is Martin Osborne." Osborne was only a middleman, but Joe wanted to hear what Arnie would say.

Joe hadn't expected him to laugh.

"Osborne's a lazy fool who thinks he's more important than he really is."

"What about Jiles Forest?"

"What about him?" Arnie stiffened.

"Some say he's in charge."

The gunman pursed his lips. "Jiles would like to think he's important."

"So someone else is in control?"

Flipping the channels on the television, Arnie stopped at the local news, sending a sickening feeling through Joe's gut. One mention of Officer Joe Petrecelli having been taken hostage and any hope Joe had of saving Callie and her brother would end.

He had to do something to force Arnie to turn the channel. Looking down at his bound hands, he realized embracing Callie's technique of peaceful harmony to affect change might be the best tactic.

"There's a Christmas special on Channel 12 based on the Nativity story," he suggested.

Arnie groaned. "I don't buy into religion."

"Neither do I, but Callie might be interested." Evidently she had some influence on Arnie, because he changed the channel to the children's story.

Callie returned, with Sanchez in tow, pushing a cart laden with serving dishes. The smell of baked turkey and all the trimmings filled the donor room. She glanced at the television and then turned a questioning gaze at Joe.

He raised his brows and shrugged.

"I heated the food in the microwave," she said, filling a plate, which she handed to Arnie.

He hesitated.

"Everything has been in the refrigerator. Away from the germs," she assured him.

He took the plate and began to eat.

Callie prepared a second serving and glanced at Joe.

He shook his head. "I'm not hungry."

"You have to eat."

"Yes, ma'am." Joe was beginning to realize that when Callie made up her mind, there was no changing course. He accepted the plate she offered and, in spite of his bound hands, managed to get the food in his mouth. The meal nourished his body and brought a renewed sense of hope to his faltering spirit.

She offered food to Malachi. He didn't eat more than a couple bites but seemed to appreciate her care and concern.

Callie was the most selfless woman Joe had ever known. Her entire focus was on others. She was even trying to change the gunmen's hearts through kindness. What was it about Callie that allowed her to be so hopeful and optimistic? Could it be her faith in God?

Joe's foster parents were believers. His foster mom told him she prayed daily for his safety. If something happened to him, he hated to think how it would affect her. His foster dad was a quiet, reserved type, but they had a good relationship. Joe wouldn't want either of them to be hurt, especially after everything they had done for him.

Callie wet one of the towels, wrung it dry and then wiped it over Malachi's forehead. He took her hand and smiled. She leaned down and whispered something in his ear. He nodded as she continued to talk to him.

Once Malachi's eyes closed, she pulled on a pair of gloves, checked her brother's leg and then walked into the other lab. Arnie was focused on the television and didn't object to her leaving. She returned with a light, which she set up to shine on Robbie's wounded calf.

"What's that for?" Sanchez asked as he piled a second helping of sweet potatoes onto his plate.

"It's a UV lamp. One of the researchers is experimenting to see how UV rays retard the growth of bacteria. If it works in the petri dish, it may work on Rocky's leg. At least that's my hope."

Once she made Robbie comfortable, Callie pulled off her gloves and washed her hands. As she returned to the corner, Joe looked up. "Fix a plate for yourself."

"I'm not hungry."

"You need to keep up your strength." He flicked his gaze to Arnie and Sanchez, both glued to the television, hoping Callie understood what he meant. The night ahead would be long. Food would sustain them both no matter what happened.

She nodded, a look of understanding on her face. She placed a few items on her plate and came back to sit next to him again.

"Were you successful?" he asked.

Her lips quirked into a hesitant grin. "Meaning?"

"Meaning the pain pills. You pocketed two

of them. I noticed you didn't put any sweet potatoes on my plate, but you gave Arnie and Sanchez double helpings. Hopefully you mixed the pain pills into their food."

Callie's face broke into a smile. "The two oxycodone would probably do the trick, but I added a couple of muscle relaxers to the potatoes, as well. One of the techs has a back problem and leaves some pills in the break room. I gave Sanchez a piece of pie to keep him occupied while I grabbed them."

She snuggled closer.

"Way to go, Callie. Now we have to wait until they fall asleep."

But Arnie and Sanchez's eyes were wide open.

Arnie's phone rang. Flipping off the television, he pushed the cell to his ear.

"Yeah?" He nodded a few times as the person on the other end spoke.

"Okay. We'll leave before dawn. Malachi's in bad shape. He might not make it through the night. Sanchez wants to head south to see if he can meet up with his family."

Arnie nodded again. "Yeah. I'll bring Rocky with me. What about the woman and the doc?"

He stared at them. "Kill both of them? Yeah. When we leave the lab."

Callie swallowed hard and laid her plate on the floor.

Joe fisted his hands. What could he do? He'd always been able to handle any bad situation and turn it to his advantage. After Theo had abandoned him as a child, Joe had vowed to always come out on top. But now, with Callie at his side and their fate in the hands of two gunmen, Joe knew this was one time he couldn't change what would happen.

With no place else to turn, he hung his head. *Lord, if you can hear me, I'm asking for Your help. Save Callie. She doesn't deserve to die. Neither does Robbie. If possible, give me an opportunity to overpower the gunmen before it's too late.*

Callie continued to check on her two patients into the night. The growth of the wound on Robbie's leg seemed to slow a bit, although she couldn't be sure. Perhaps she was imagining the slight improvement.

Malachi wasn't faring well. Blood oozed from the wound whenever he moved. Callie started another unit of blood, but his red blood count remained low when she ran a second CBC.

"Malachi, you need to keep fighting. Don't

give up." She bent close to his ear. "You want to see your mama."

He moaned and grabbed her hand. "Don't… don't tell her…what… I done. I… I didn't mean to hurt no one."

"Ask God to forgive you, Malachi. He loves you."

"I wanna get right with the Lord. Cross my heart. Say a prayer for me."

"We'll pray together." Callie held his hand, and began to pray.

"There's something I need to tell you," he said when the prayer ended. Callie leaned down once again and listened as the youngest gunman bared his soul. When he finished, she drew the blanket over his chest. He smiled feebly and mouthed "thank you."

Wetting a second towel, Callie sponged Robbie's hot forehead. She took his temperature. The thermometer registered 104 degrees. Sadness wrapped around her.

The overhead fluorescent lights glared in her eyes. Needing to focus on life rather than death, Callie lowered the switch, leaving only a small light on near the doorway.

She plugged in the lights to the Christmas tree. The tiny colorful bulbs flickered on and off, catching Robbie's eyes. His lips twitched ever so slightly, as if he enjoyed seeing the tree aglow.

Callie glanced at the wall clock. Almost midnight. Just a few more minutes and it would be Christmas. No matter what happened, they needed to celebrate the birth of the Christ Child.

Feeling someone's gaze, she turned. Joe stared at her from across the room. Callie's cheeks warmed. Even his spirits seemed buoyed by the Christmas lights. She clicked on a small CD player that sat on the shelf against the wall, and the soothing sounds of Christmas music played.

Arnie turned off the television and watched as she pulled a Bible from one of the drawers and padded across the lab back to where Joe sat. Lowering herself to the floor, she stared at the clock until the two hands pointed to twelve.

Opening the Bible, she began to read with a strong, clear voice from the beginning of Luke's gospel. "In those days, Caesar Augustus published a decree ordering a census of the whole world…"

Joe tipped his head back and closed his eyes.

Arnie and Sanchez listened as she read. Even Malachi seemed to understand the significance of the story.

Robbie calmed, and his face filled with peace. The UV light streamed down on his leg, like the star that had hovered over the tiny stable.

"While they were there the days of her confinement were completed. She gave birth to her first-born son and wrapped him in swaddling clothes and laid him in a manger…"

More than two thousand years ago, Joseph had tried to find shelter for his pregnant wife soon to give birth, but there had been no room in the inn. Did Callie have room in her heart for the Lord? Or did she have a Do Not Enter sign nailed across the entryway? She'd closed her door to Robbie, and he'd ended up with the Exterminators.

As she read, she glanced from one gunman to the next. Had doors closed on them long ago? Is that why they had chosen the darkness of a life of crime instead of the light of Christ? When she finished the narrative, she shut the Bible and listened to the soft strains of the Christmas music.

Digging a cell phone from his pocket, Sanchez slid from the chair. "I'm gonna call my wife." He stepped into the larger laboratory. "*Hola,* Maria? *Feliz Navidad.*"

Hopefully the message had gotten through

to him. What about Arnie? Would the Christmas story affect him in a positive way? Or was he the same man who had shoved Callie along the laboratory corridor earlier today? *Lord, change his heart, and help us stay alive.*

Chapter Eleven

Callie watched Arnie wrap his arms across his chest and stare at the ceiling. No telling what he was thinking.

Joe's fingers touched her arm. "The Scripture made me remember the real meaning of Christmas."

She smiled at him, seeing the warmth in his gaze. "Amazing, isn't it? Christ came as a child born so long ago, yet the Christmas message holds the power to heal troubled hearts even today. All of us need to hear that message and allow it to transform our lives."

He scooted closer to her. "There's something I need to tell you, Callie. It's about your brother."

She shook her head. "I don't want to hear about jail time or years in prison today, Joe.

It's hard enough knowing I'm the reason he strayed."

"You?" He looked surprised. "But you told him to make something of himself."

"A lot of good that did."

"You're wrong, Callie. What you said to Robbie caused him to change. That's what I needed to tell you. Robbie's not part of the gang. He infiltrated the Exterminators as an undercover cop."

She shook her head, confused by what Joe had just said. "He's a cop? Why didn't you tell me, Joe?"

"Because one slip and—"

"One slip? You didn't trust me?"

"Of course I trusted you, but I was responsible for your brother's safety. I'm the one who insisted he be moved to Lazarus House. I got him and both of us into this mess."

All this time, Callie had felt responsible for her brother's actions.

"You gave your brother a mandate to change," Joe continued. "Your tough love opened his eyes. He told me he cleaned up his life because of what Callie had told him. I didn't realize the Callie he was talking about was his sister."

"Rob… Robbie said my words made a difference?"

Joe nodded. "The problem isn't with Robbie, is it? The problem is with you. You still can't forgive yourself."

Joe was right. She'd carried the guilt for her sister's death and Robbie's failures for too long.

"You believe in the Lord," Joe said. "Don't you believe He forgives?"

"Of course I do."

"But you can't accept that forgiveness in your own life."

"You should talk."

Callie had prayed with Theo, asking the Lord to change Joe's heart. The man who now questioned her ability to forgive should look more closely at himself. Scripture said it was easier to see a splinter in another's eye rather than the plank in one's own eye. That Biblical message certainly applied to Joe.

"I need to check on my brother." Callie couldn't think, sitting so close to Joe. She needed space and time alone. Robbie was a cop? The words she'd said to him three years ago had made a difference in his life? Was Joe telling her the truth?

She took the damp cloth and wiped her brother's brow. His forehead felt even hotter than before. Surely, he couldn't survive much longer with the aggressive infection eating away his flesh. *Please, Lord, let him live.*

She moved to Malachi's side. He needed to be sponged off, as well and his dressing changed, but that might not be enough. Just like for her brother, this Christmas could be Malachi's last.

Sanchez ended his conversation with his wife and came back into the donor room, his bravado somewhat mellowed. "I talked to Maria."

Arnie looked in his direction. "So?"

"So the kids want to know when their dad's coming home. I'm leaving soon."

"I don't like it."

"It's Christmas, man. Don't you have family?"

Arnie rubbed his jaw. "Not anymore."

"Parents?"

"I left home a long time ago and never looked back." He shook his head. "We were dirt-poor. No money. Not enough food. The only thing different about Christmas was a little candy on our dinner plates."

"What about church?"

The ringleader laughed. "Church? The only

time I went was on my wedding day." He shrugged. "My wife said old habits die hard. When she left, she took the baby. Now I've got money but no one to spend it on." He chortled. "Maybe I'll buy gifts for your kids, Sanchez. How many you got?"

"Five. One on the way."

Joe listened as the gunmen talked. Sad to think of the bad choices they had each made. What about his own choices? As a thirteen-year-old, he'd reacted the only way he knew how. If something hurt, cut it out of your life. Theo hadn't wanted him. Stood to reason that Joe wouldn't want Theo, either.

But years had passed, and the fast living that had been Theo's reason for closing his door to Joe had done damage. Because of the cancer, his brother's medical condition was fragile at best. Yet the two of them had never reconnected.

Forgiveness? The word flickered through Joe's mind. He'd told Callie to forgive herself. Truth was, Joe needed to forgive Theo.

Something he couldn't do.

Callie wiped a cloth over Malachi's forehead and lowered her ear as he whispered something to her. Adjusting the blanket around his shoulders, she patted his hand and then went back to her brother and once again examined his leg. The wound had grown.

Callie's face was drawn as she returned to the corner and sat a few feet away.

Joe was filled with regret. "I didn't tell you about your brother, Callie, because I wanted to keep you safe," he whispered as Arnie and Sanchez talked.

"You didn't trust me."

"I didn't know you, Callie. We only met a few hours ago." He looked into the depth of her soul and saw the purity and beauty of this woman he'd been waiting his whole lifetime to find. "Now it seems like I've known you forever."

"Did you give Robbie the undercover assignment?"

Joe nodded, knowing he had to tell her everything, even if it would turn her against him for good.

"Your brother asked to infiltrate the Exterminators, but the decision to use him was mine. He's made a difference, Callie. His actions have been courageous and self-sacrificing. That's who he became after you challenged him to grow into a man."

"I told him I'd pray for him to be the man God had created him to be."

"Your prayers paid off. Robbie's a fine and noble person. A person I'm proud to know."

Tears swelled in her eyes, and she scooted closer. Placing her hand in his, the two of them sat for a long moment. "You know Theo loves you," Callie finally said.

Joe's throat thickened.

"Theo said his life was mixed up when your parents died. He was into things he didn't want you to know about. That's why he didn't take you in. He wanted something better for you."

"Better?" Joe thought of his foster parents and the brick two-story house where they lived—a place he now called home. Good people, they had given him love and acceptance, guidance and respect. Under their care, he had moved from a troubled adolescence into a stable adulthood.

Joe tipped his head back. His eyes rested on the hand-hewn stable where the ceramic figures of Joseph and Mary gathered around the manger. *Peace on earth, goodwill toward men.* The words played through his mind. Maybe he could at least have goodwill toward his brother. It would be a start.

Callie squeezed his hand. "You've been doing a very good thing, and it's probably

worth more because of the way you feel about
Theo."

"Worth more? What do you mean?"

"You're his anonymous donor, aren't you?
Tamika mentioned that someone paid Theo's
bills, but she never told me it was his estranged
brother. Theo doesn't even know."

"It needs to stay that way. It wouldn't do any
good for him to know his younger brother is
supporting him."

"Probably not. But you're a good man, Joe.
Theo's lucky to have you in his life."

Joe looked into her eyes as their fingers entwined. "If I've learned anything during this
hostage situation, Callie, it's that life can't be
taken for granted. Certain things are important, like relationships and family and someone to love."

Chapter Twelve

Joe watched the two gunmen for some sign of fatigue. Callie had mixed the pain medication in with the sweet potato casserole, which the men had eaten, yet neither appeared tired.

"We need to leave," Sanchez said. "The middle of the night is our best chance to get out of the city."

Arnie nodded. "But I say when."

Grumbling, Sanchez retreated back to the donor chair. Settling into the contour, he closed his eyes and soon fell asleep. At least the medication had worked on one of the gunmen.

Callie padded quietly to Malachi's side. Once again, she wiped his hands and brow then bent down to whisper in his ear. One lone tear fell from his eye and rolled down the side of his face.

Before long, the Exterminators would claim another fatality. Heaviness settled over Joe. *Lord, no more deaths. Protect us from harm.*

Callie checked her brother's leg and wiped his forehead. Robbie's eyes blinked open. He raised his hand off the bed and pointed to the crèche. She smiled and nodded.

The action between brother and sister signaled reconciliation and forgiveness. Callie's face reflected love and acceptance. Robbie, even through his fever and pain, seemed renewed, as if the action brought healing.

Joe's eyes fell on the tiny manger and the babe who came so that all might have eternal life.

Malachi? Would he see the face of God?

Robbie? *Oh, Lord, he needs medical care. Keep him alive.*

And Callie? *Keep her safe.*

Take me instead, Lord.

Callie came back to the corner and sat next to Joe. Without having to ask, she whispered, "Robbie and I used to act out the Nativity when we were young. He liked to pretend he was the lamb following the shepherd to the stable."

"The shepherd—the Good Shepherd—protected him from harm," Joe said aloud.

Surprise registered on her face. "That's

right. He always asked God to protect both of us when our parents argued."

"Protected by a God who loved you," Joe added. Hearing his own voice made the words real to him.

Had it only been hours since he and Callie had met? He loved her courage, her determination, her optimism. Fact was, he was starting to love Callie.

She wouldn't let anyone control her life nor would she back down about her relationship with the Lord. Joe wanted that confidence in a loving God as well.

"Pray with me," he whispered. "I want the fullness of God's love."

Tears filled her eyes. "He already lives within you, Joe. You just didn't recognize Him."

Callie placed her hand in his and prayed with him. Love filled his heart like he'd never known before. Love for Callie. Love for the Lord.

He finally saw clearly. Theo hadn't abandoned him all those years ago. He'd made a decision about what would be best for Joe. Tough love.

As a young teen, Joe had only thought about his immediate pain. He hadn't thought about needing a good home life and stability, which is what his foster parents had provided. If Joe hadn't shut Theo out of his life, perhaps the loving family that had raised Joe and provided for his every need could have influenced his brother. Instead, Joe had excluded Theo.

If only he had a chance to ask his brother's forgiveness. From the depths of his heart, Joe knew the Lord forgave him. Now if only he'd have the opportunity to ask Theo's forgiveness.

Arnie stood and turned on the overhead television. He flipped the channels to the all-night news. The order of stories appeared in a sidebar on the screen. The Atlanta hostage segment was next in the lineup.

Malachi moaned.

"You think he caught Rocky's infection?" Arnie asked Sanchez, but he was still asleep.

Squeezing Joe's hand, Callie whispered, "This might be what we've been waiting for. I'll try to get into the micro lab and come up with some type of disruption. I grabbed vinegar and baking soda from the break room. It'll sound worse than it really is."

Arnie motioned Callie toward him. "My throat hurts," he said as she neared. "You think I could have that flesh-eating bug?"

Callie hesitated, throwing a quick glance

back at Joe. "I'm not sure. Let me do a throat culture." She pulled a sterile swab from a drawer. "Open your mouth."

Arnie complied. While she swabbed his throat, Joe pulled the debriding scissors from his pocket and snipped through the tie that bound his hands.

"I'll test this right away." Callie headed for the micro lab.

Holding his hands together as if they were still bound, Joe stood up.

Arnie glared at him. "What are you doing?"

"I need to stretch my legs."

"Forget it."

"Really, Arnie. My legs are stiff. I just need to stand."

"I said no."

Robbie jerked, knocking the UV light to the floor. Joe leaned down to pick up the lamp and unplugged the cord at the same time.

Callie stepped back into the donor room. "I've got bad news, Arnie. You've got the same infection as Rocky."

The ringleader raised his hands and clutched his neck. His eyes widened.

Knowing she was setting Arnie up, Joe prepared to act.

Sanchez blinked his eyes open and stared at

the television screen as the news report continued.

"Law enforcement provided a photo of the Atlanta police officer thought to have been taken hostage," the newscaster said. "His name is Joe Petrecelli."

Joe's picture flashed on the screen.

"Yikes, Arnie." Sanchez slid out of his chair and pointed to Joe. "He's a cop."

Behind them, an explosion tore through the micro lab.

Arnie and Sanchez turned toward the doorway.

"Fire," Callie screamed, grabbing the extinguisher from the wall.

In one swift motion, she pulled the pin and aimed the flow of retardant at Sanchez. The spray hit him in the face, knocking him back against the counter. His head hit the overhead cabinet.

She slammed the canister against his chest. With a loud moan, Sanchez doubled over and slid to the floor.

Joe struck Arnie with the metal base of the UV lamp as he fumbled for his gun. The rapid motion tore at Joe's wound, and pain, hot as lightning, ricocheted down his arm.

Arnie pulled his weapon free. Turning, he

aimed at Callie. She readjusted the canister in her hands, oblivious to the immediate danger.

Joe had to save her. Gathering strength from deep within him, he lurched forward, slamming his good shoulder into Arnie's side. Air wheezed from the gunman's lungs. Joe grabbed his wrist, and the two men fought for control of the automatic.

"No," Callie screamed. She raised the extinguisher and slammed it against Arnie's head.

Staggering backward, he crashed into the biohazard trash container, knocking it over as he fell to the floor. The gun dropped, and the contents of the receptacle spilled onto Arnie's lap.

He covered his face with his hands and screamed.

Joe grabbed the gun and aimed it at Arnie. "Call the police, Callie. Tell them we've got the Exterminators under control."

Chapter Thirteen

Callie stood at Robbie's bedside, praying that the massive doses of antibiotics threading through his veins would combat the flesh-eating strep. When they'd arrived at the hospital in the middle of the night, the doctors hadn't been optimistic. Now as the sun began to set on Christmas Day, Callie felt especially discouraged and alone.

A knock at the door caused her to raise her eyes. "Come in."

Her heart fluttered as Joe stepped into the room. His arm was in a sling, his eye had swollen shut and a large bandage covered his neck, but he looked more handsome than ever.

In his good arm, he carried a small artificial Christmas tree decorated with tiny lights and shiny ornaments.

"I thought you could use a little cheering up." He placed the tree on a table in the corner and pushed a switch.

"Battery operated and hospital friendly." The lights flickered, sending colorful spots dancing along the walls.

"It's beautiful, Joe."

Stepping to Callie's side, he rubbed his hand over her shoulder and stared down at her brother. "Any change?"

"Not that I can tell. They drew another CBC a short while ago. The nurse said she'd let me know his white blood count once she hears from the lab."

"Why don't you take a break, Callie? I'll stay with Robbie."

She shook her head. "No, I need to be here."

"You've got to be exhausted."

"I'm okay, Joe."

"Which is what you always say. I do have some good news. Tamika and the police guard are stable and should make full recoveries."

"Oh, that's wonderful."

"I met Tamika's husband and girls in the hallway outside her room. They said they're praying for Robbie."

"That's what he needs right now. Did you find out about Malachi?"

"He made it through surgery, and the doctors expect him to pull through. His mother and grandmother were relieved."

"Did you tell them he'd have to stand trial?"

"No, not yet. That discussion can wait until after Christmas. Sanchez and Arnie are being questioned, although it's doubtful either of them will divulge the name of the man at the top." Callie heard discouragement in Joe's voice. "The Exterminators won't be stopped until their leader is apprehended."

"His name's Sanders Brown."

"What?"

"Malachi thought he was going to die and wanted to come clean. He told me Brown was in charge of the Exterminators. I should have mentioned it sooner, but after everything that happened, it slipped my mind."

"Oh, Callie, you are amazing."

Another knock sounded and the door opened. A nurse peered into the room. "The lab called. Robbie's white blood count has dropped a bit."

Relief swept over Callie.

"What's that mean?" Joe asked.

"It means the antibiotics are working," she explained.

"He's not out of the woods yet," the nurse added. "But there's improvement."

"Which is what I've been praying for." Callie waved her thanks as the nurse left the room.

Joe wrapped his arm around Callie. She felt Joe's strength once again and was uplifted by his presence. They'd been through so much in the last thirty-six hours. It seemed they'd been together for a lifetime, which is what she hoped might unfold for their future. Of course, she didn't know how Joe felt. Things would be different once they both went back to their normal workday routines. Not knowing what tomorrow would bring, she closed her eyes, wanting to hold on to this moment forever.

"Callie?"

She looked down. Her brother's eyes were opened.

"I... I'm sorry," he whispered.

"Don't worry about anything right now, Robbie. The antibiotics are working, and you're going to get better." Callie was sure the Lord had heard and was answering her prayer.

"I... I was wrong, Callie. Mixed-up. Dad had died. And Mom."

"Shhh," she soothed. "We all make mistakes. I shouldn't have closed my door to you three years ago, Robbie. Then I thought you had joined the Exterminators. Joe told me your were working undercover."

Her brother tried to smile as he looked at Joe. "How are you, sir?"

"Better now that you're getting the medical care you need. Oh, and by the way, I think your sister's the greatest."

Callie's heart went into overdrive, but she knew the offhanded remark was only a figure of speech.

"So do I," Robbie said.

Tears burned her eyes. She'd wanted to hear something positive from her brother for so long.

"There's something I need to tell you," Robbie said, his voice growing stronger. "I was cleaning out some old letters and things of Dad's after he died. One letter was addressed to Mom."

"Written after they divorced?"

Robbie nodded. "But he never mailed it. Dad wrote that he had been working on the gate the morning Becky died. He'd taken out a bolt on the latch and should have replaced it, but he'd gotten distracted since it was Christmas. The latch looked like it would work but sprung open when any weight pushed against it. He said he was to blame for Becky wandering off."

All these years, Callie had carried the guilt for her sister's death. "Why didn't he mail the letter to Mom?"

"Maybe he thought she wouldn't forgive him."

Forgiveness. Callie hadn't been able to forgive herself. She'd missed so much in life because of the guilt that had eaten into her like the flesh-eating strep had eaten into Robbie's leg.

This Christmas was the time for new beginnings. She wanted to put all the pain and guilt behind her and start fresh. Joe's hand was on her shoulder. She reached out and entwined her fingers with his.

Once again the door opened and a young woman stepped inside. She was pretty with long blond hair and big blue eyes. "Robbie?"

Haltingly, she stepped toward the bed. "I just found out what happened." Tears spilled down her cheeks.

He took her outstretched hand. "Everything's going to be okay, Missy."

She kissed his forehead then wiped her hand over her face and smiled at Callie. "You must be Robbie's sister. He's talked so much about you. I'm Missy Adams. Robbie and I are—"

She smiled down at him.

"Planning to get married," Robbie completed her sentence. "That's why I wanted to see you, Callie. So you and Missy could meet."

Seeing the love so evident in her brother's eyes when he looked at Missy, Callie knew he would have a complete recovery. She and Missy would get to know each other in the days ahead, but right now, the young couple needed a bit of privacy.

Joe took Callie's hand as they moved to the corner. "In spite of everything that happened, this is the best Christmas of my life," he said.

She turned to face him.

A warm glow tingled her neck.

"I don't want this to end, Callie." He rubbed his fingers over hers. "I want every day to be Christmas. Not the hostage part, of course, but being together. I want to see you tomorrow and the next day and the next. I want to call you from work and tell you how my day went when my shift's over. I want to share birthdays and holidays and go to church with you every Sunday."

Her head swirled and she wanted to laugh

with joy. "Aren't you moving a little fast, Officer Petrecelli?"

"Hmmm? Maybe. But who knows what the future holds?"

A life together was her dream, and she was beginning to think it was Joe's, as well.

He hesitated for a moment then glanced at Robbie and his girlfriend. Callie followed his gaze. The young couple was totally occupied.

"I stopped by Lazarus House this afternoon," Joe finally said.

"Room ten?"

He nodded. "I told Theo I'd met a very special woman. I said I didn't deserve you, and that we must have met because of his prayers. Then I asked his forgiveness for closing him out of my life. Only he said he was the one who'd been wrong."

Callie sighed with contentment as Joe wrapped his arm around her and drew her close. Being careful of his wounded shoulder, she snuggled into his embrace and, without hesitation, raised her lips to meet his. Their kiss was long and lingering and filled with the promise of a lifetime of Christmases to come.

The tree twinkled, bathing them in light, but it was the light of Christ, the light of a child born so long ago, that reflected in their hearts.

Forgiveness and reconciliation, healing and wholeness were all wrapped up in the Christmas message. Callie's heart sang with joy, and in the distance she heard a joyous chorus as if the angels were singing on high: "Peace on earth. Goodwill toward men."

* * * * *

Dear Reader,

Emotions intensify at Christmas. For most people, the holidays are a time of joy. For others, they are bittersweet, often shadowed by pain and loss. The good news is that Christ came into the world to bring light to the darkness. Writing *Yule Die* allowed me to explore how a baby born in a manger more than 2,000 years ago can transform lives for the better today.

Callie and Joe learned the true meaning of Christmas in *Yule Die* and in so doing found love and happiness. Once they were able to ask and receive forgiveness, they were freed from the pain of their pasts. By turning to the Lord, they allowed the light of Christ to shine in the darkness.

If you're suffering and in pain, ask the Lord to touch your life in a new and special way. Open your heart to the message of love freely given. By embracing the true meaning of the season, you'll find transformation and healing.

I'd love to hear from you. E-mail me at debby@debbygiusti.com.

To learn about my other books, visit me online at www.DebbyGiusti.com.

Merry Christmas!

Wishing you abundant blessing,

Debby Giusti

Questions for Discussion

1. Why does the news report about the shoot-out in Atlanta trouble Callie at the onset of the story?

2. Callie believes Christmas should be a time of joy instead of sorrow, yet her own life hasn't been especially happy. What does Callie believe about Christmas that makes the difference in her life?

3. What does her association with Lazarus House tell us about the real Callie Evans?

4. Joe believes Callie uses peaceful harmony to effect change. How does she put that into action throughout the story?

5. Why can't Joe forgive his brother? Is his struggle with Theo justified in your opinion?

6. What does Joe finally realize about Theo? Why do you think the older brother turned his back on Joe when he was thirteen? Do you think there might be more than one reason?

7. Neither Joe nor Callie had anyone who would come looking for them on Christmas Eve. Is that telling? If so, what do we know about both of them, at least at the beginning of the story?

8. What secret do we learn about Joe in regard to his brother? What does that tell us about the real Joe Petrecelli?